DARK HOURS

© 2006 by Gudrun Pausewang
English translation © 2006 by John Brownjohn
Text of the original German edition: Überleben!
Copyright © 2005, Ravensburger Buchverlag Otto Maier GmbH, Ravensburg (Germany)

Annick Press Ltd.

Copyedited by Elizabeth McLean
Proofread by Melissa Edwards
Cover and interior design by Irvin Cheung/iCheung Design
Photo, p. iv: A German woman carrying her few possessions runs from a burning building in Seigburg, Germany, 1945. © US National Archives and Records Administration

Cataloging in Publication
Pausewang, Gudrun
      Dark hours / written by Gudrun Pausewang ; translated by
John Brownjohn.

Translation of: Überleben!
ISBN-10: 1-55451-042-2
ISBN-13: 978-1-55451-042-9

      I. Brownjohn, John II. Title.
PT2676.A94U3413 2006   833'.914   C2006-901795-6

Printed and bound in Canada

Published in the U.S.A. by	**Distributed in Canada by**	**Distributed in the U.S.A. by**
Annick Press (U.S.) Ltd.	Firefly Books Ltd.	Firefly Books (U.S.) Inc.
	66 Leek Crescent	P.O. Box 1338
	Richmond Hill, ON	Ellicott Station
	L4B 1H1	Buffalo, NY 14205

Visit our website at **www.annickpress.com**

DARK HOURS

Gudrun Pausewang

Translated by John Brownjohn

annick press
toronto + new york + vancouver

Germany's Dark Hours

ANYONE READING A BOOK about an event that occurred during World War Two (1939–45) should know how that terrible conflict started and how it turned out.

WORLD WAR ONE (1914–18) ENDED IN THE DEFEAT of Germany and the creation of the Treaty of Versailles, which imposed harsh conditions on that country. Forced to repay the cost of the war, the German economy was in ruins. While the rest of post-war Europe slowly began to recover from the devastating economic effects of the conflict, Germany faced high inflation, which drove the cost of food and other goods sky-high. Citizens were deeply troubled about the future of their country.

In addition to the economic hardship that followed war's end, the Versailles Treaty also gave some German provinces, where the first language and cultural heritage were predominantly German, to France, Czechoslovakia and Poland. This added to the feeling of humiliation. The combination of grievances that followed in the wake of the First World War helped set the stage for what was to come.

Adolf Hitler, an Austrian who had fought for Germany, dreamed of uniting all ethnic Germans under a single flag. Disappointed and disillusioned by Germany's defeat like countless other war veterans, Hitler went to live in Munich, Germany. There he joined a small political party whose nationalistic platform was in agreement with his ideas. This was the NSDAP (National Socialist German Labor Party, commonly known as the Nazi Party).

In 1921, Hitler rose to become leader of the Nazi Party and ensured that all its members obeyed him without question from then on. The party's main aim was to create a Greater Germany whose frontiers would expand to include the ethnic German areas in the east and regain Germany's status as a great power. Taking advantage of an existing undercurrent of anti-Semitism, which had been strong throughout Europe even before the rise of Nazism, the Nazi Party used the Jews as scapegoats for all of Germany's economic woes.

After electoral setbacks, Hitler's party became the largest in the German government. In his speeches he restored the people's sense of national pride, and glorified all things German. To an impoverished nation with mass unemployment, he held out the prospect of work and a better life.

In 1933, Hitler became Chancellor of Germany, the nation's second most important political position. Almost immediately, he proceeded to carry out his plans. Banning all other parties and establishing a dictatorship, he put millions of unemployed men to work on the autobahns, or motorways, with an eye to their strategic value in a future war. He also built up a powerful new army, navy and air force in defiance of the terms of the Versailles Treaty.

Joseph Goebbels, the Nazi minister of propaganda, saw to it that Hitler (known as the Führer, or "Leader," from 1934 on) became a cult figure to be revered with almost religious fervor. Innumerable Nazi Party rallies fanned the flames of German patriotism with the aid of fluttering banners, smart uniforms, warlike songs, mass parades and torchlight processions. Indoctrinated by the media and the Nazi youth movement, German children and adolescents were brought up to be loyal young Nazis by their schoolteachers and, in many cases, by their own parents.

In March 1938, Hitler sent German troops into Austria, his homeland, and incorporated it into what the Nazis called the Greater German Reich, or German Empire. By March 1939, his army occupied all of Czechoslovakia as well.

WORLD WAR TWO WAS DELIBERATELY PLANNED and unleashed by Hitler, who invaded Poland on September 1, 1939. Britain and France, bound by treaty to assist the Poles if they were attacked, declared war on Germany two days later. In the spring of 1940, German troops occupied Denmark and Norway. May 10, 1940 saw the start of the so-called Blitzkrieg, a lightning-fast campaign in the course of which the German armies swept through Luxembourg, Holland and Belgium, and defeated France within six weeks. That summer, Hitler drove through the streets of Berlin in triumph, cheered by enthusiastic crowds.

Beginning in the fall of 1940, Germany also mounted aggressive nighttime bombing missions on London and other urban centers in Great Britain. This was known as the Blitz.

From 1941 on, any Jews who had not escaped from Germany and German-occupied territory were forced to wear a yellow Star of David on their chest. In what became known as the "Final Solution," the first extermination camps were established with the purpose of killing as many Jews as possible. Sadly, most Germans shut their eyes to the atrocities committed by the Nazi regime against Jews, gypsies, Jehovah's Witnesses (and other religious groups), homosexuals, and people with physical or mental disabilities. Even today, many Germans who grew up under Hitler claim to have known nothing about the persecution of the Jews during his twelve years in power. They say that it was not until after the war that they learned of the extermination camps where Jews were murdered on a positively industrial scale.

These people are being less than honest. I myself was only seventeen years old when the war and the Nazi era ended, but even I was aware that any Jews who had not fled Germany were in mortal danger. Like most Germans, I did not know that they were being killed so systematically, but we all realized they were targets of the Nazi regime. Those who claim to have been ignorant of these things are only trying to avoid their share of blame for a gross injustice.

ON JUNE 22, 1941, Hitler invaded the former Soviet Union in violation of his non-aggression pact with Soviet leader Joseph Stalin.

The German armies advanced rapidly but ground to a halt outside Moscow in December of that year. In the same month, blinded to the fact that his ambition was surpassing his military strength, Hitler declared war on the United States as well.

When the British and Americans launched air raids on major German cities in 1942, it marked an unmistakable turning point in the war. In Stalingrad, in the Soviet Union, 220,000 German men were either killed or taken captive. Despite the freezing cold, lack of food, and encirclement by the Soviet army, Hitler had refused his general's request to allow his troops to withdraw. The Germans' faith in Hitler's invincibility began to wane.

From 1943 on, German armies were forced to retreat on all fronts. The Allies intensified air raids on German cities. Still, trainloads of Jews continued to be transported eastward, bound for the extermination camps in Poland.

In June 1944, British, Canadian and American troops landed on the French coast and proceeded to push inland. Some German army officers staged an unsuccessful attempt on Hitler's life. Hitler immediately ordered a search for the conspirators. Thousands were arrested, while 200 were executed for the failed assassination.

By early 1945, the end of the war was in sight. In the east, German refugees began to stream westward to escape the advancing Russians. Thousands died en route.

IN THIS BOOK, Gisela Beck and her mother, brothers and grandmother are fleeing from the Russians, having left their home and all their possessions behind. They travel west by train in an attempt to reach the comparative safety of Dresden, where some of their relatives are living, but have to change trains at a town along the way.

Formerly one of the most beautiful cities in Germany and famous for its art and architecture, Dresden was destroyed by Allied bombers on February 13–14, 1945.

After fighting their way across France, Allied troops crossed the German frontier early in March. On April 30, Hitler committed suicide, and on May 8 the carnage finally ended. Many millions of people had lost their lives.

WE GERMANS SHOULD NEVER HAVE ALLOWED Hitler to come to power, nor, once he had done so, should we have allowed him to plan and start a war. He had quite openly stated in his book *Mein Kampf* (My Struggle), which was published back in the 1920s, that he intended to rid Germany of Jews and acquire more "living space" by military means. That prediction was down on paper for anyone to read.

Monstrous crimes were committed in my country's name. We cannot undo those crimes or turn back the clock; we can only do our utmost to ensure that no new dictator gains a hold over us, leads us into a war, and persecutes, torments and annihilates our fellow creatures, no matter what their race or religion. The history of Germany during the twentieth century should be a lesson to people of all nations.

– GUDRUN PAUSEWANG

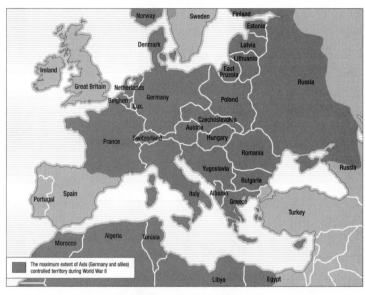

The maximum extent of Axis (Germany and allies) controlled territory during World War II

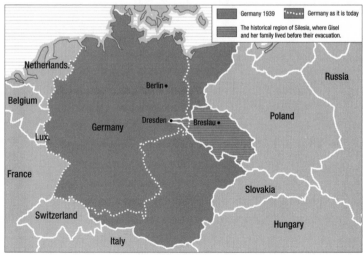

Germany 1939

Germany as it is today

The historical region of Silesia, where Gisel and her family lived before their evacuation.

February 5

Dear Stefanie,

It's your sixteenth birthday tomorrow. I was wondering some months ago what to give you. A purse? A pair of roller blades? A cell phone? No, you already have all those.

So I decided to give you something money can't buy—something as unique as that picture you painted for me.

I hit on the idea of writing a story that may interest you: the story of my own sixteenth birthday. Writing it wasn't easy. There were times when I wept as I dug out all the memories that had been slumbering for decades in the innermost recesses of my mind, some of which I didn't want to remember.

It's a true story. I lived it myself, sixty long years ago. I was your age then. Sixteen plus sixty is seventy-six—my present age.

You've been luckier than me. So far, all you've known is peace. I had to learn the meaning of war, and not only from newspapers or the radio. I experienced its violence and brutality first hand.

My birthday wish is that you be spared such experiences, and that my story will help you to understand me more deeply and bring us even closer together.

Your loving Grandmother

1

"You stay here with the boys, Gisel!" Granny calls to me. "And keep an eye on our luggage, you hear? Conditions like these are a thieves' paradise!" She turns to me once more and adds, "Don't let the little ones out of your sight. I'm relying on you!"

I give her a nod and make a grab for my brother Harald, who has spotted a big parrot in a cage on top of a heap of suitcases and wants to take a closer look. I shake my head at him. It's too risky in a crowd like this.

"I'm relying on you..." Mummy told me the same thing this morning, when we said goodbye on the platform at—what was the name of the station?

So here I am, sitting on a suitcase with my baby brother Rolfi on my lap. He whimpers and struggles to get down. I let him slither to the ground but keep hold of his hand. He tries to free himself and toddle after Granny. She's hurrying across the big station concourse to the information desk to ask when the next train for Dresden leaves. I try to keep my eyes on her, but she elbows her way into the crowd and disappears. I stand on tiptoe and search for a glimpse of Granny's gray hair. It's no use. There are people everywhere, hurrying about, shouting to each other, or just waiting, like us. I hope they don't all want to go to Dresden. Mummy's parents, Grandpa and Grandma Glottke, live in Dresden. That's where we're headed, all five of us.

All six, actually. Or, to be exact, all seven.

I've got such a headache. My thoughts are in a whirl too—they drift along, flitting from this to that. Memories keep surfacing in my mind, one after another. Everything was so sudden and moved so fast. So much has happened in the last twenty-four hours, I still haven't caught up properly, still haven't taken it in. I need to think over all that has happened since the day before yesterday and straighten it out in my mind, but how can I in this pandemonium?

"I only want to see the parrot close up," Harald pleads. "Please!"

Rolfi has started yowling. I hoist him onto my lap again and glance at the big clock over the entrance to the platforms. Twelve minutes to one. This time yesterday we were still at home.

YESTERDAY WE WERE AT HOME, but our world had been turned upside down since nine that morning. We guessed what old Kahlwinkel was bringing us when we caught sight of him through the kitchen window.

Mummy cast a horrified glance at Granny, who nodded and said, "Looks as if the time has come…"

She had been expecting the evacuation order for weeks now, and wondering why it still hadn't come. Well, now it had. The mayor had sent Kahlwinkel, the village messenger, hurrying from house to house with the directive from district headquarters, so that people would have a few hours in which to get their bare necessities together.

Kahlwinkel insisted on reading the document aloud to us. He read as loudly as if he were addressing a public meeting—and so slowly that Granny lost patience with him, snatched the sheet of paper from his hand and read out the essential points. We were instructed to present ourselves at the nearest railway station at four that afternoon, which meant leaving the house at three. That gave us six-and-a-half hours in which to decide what we could take with us, what would have to be left behind, and what to do with our animals.

Six-and-a-half hours...An absurdly short time in which to get used to the idea of going away and leaving nearly everything dear to us behind.

Not just the house and garden, the dog kennel and rabbit hutch, the woodshed and hen-coop. The furniture and pictures, as well, and the curtains and carpets, and the smell of the rooms and the view from the windows—everything that was so familiar to us: our home.

We couldn't even salvage what was in the cupboards and chests of drawers or on the shelves. My favorite books, the doll I'm still fond of although it's ages since I played with her, the brand-new ice skates I'd always wanted and had finally been given for Christmas, only a few weeks ago—everything had to be left behind.

We were permitted to take only as much as we could carry. Harald is six and Rolfi's just eighteen months, so they're too little to carry anything and Mummy couldn't manage much in her present condition, so all we took were three suitcases, a small backpack and a big traveling bag. We stuffed them as full as we could.

Those five pieces of luggage held all our possessions. Not our favorite things, either, but only what we would need for the journey. "For our survival," as Mummy put it, but Granny contradicted her. "You're exaggerating," she said. "The Red Cross people will provide us with all we need at the stations en route. Besides, I'm sure we'll be back before long…"

Damn and blast this war! It's wrong to swear, I know, but I can't think of anything more appropriate to say. If it were peacetime we wouldn't have had to leave everything behind. If it were peacetime we wouldn't have had to abandon our home and our village in such a rush. If it weren't for the war, the Russians wouldn't have occupied most of our province of Silesia. Then Silesia would still be a nice, peaceful, friendly part of Germany.

The war must be an especially bad one. "The First World War was nothing compared to this…" That's what our neighbor, Grandpa Häusler, kept saying these last few months, and he should know, having been all through the First World War from start to finish.

"We oughtn't to be surprised," Granny grumbled yesterday while we were packing. "We Germans started the war. Hitler was positively itching for it, and we gave him all the support he needed. We cheered him on—we, the German people. Well, now it's payback time…"

Six months ago Mummy used to get angry whenever Granny said such things, but yesterday she simply let her run on. She was probably feeling too tired and depressed to get worked up about it.

Rolfi has fallen asleep because I've been jiggling him up and down on my knee. I get to my feet again and scan the crowd for any sign of Granny. Nothing. There are too many people fighting their way to the counters, grimly pushing and shoving as they force a path through the crush.

"Look, now they're taking it away!" Harald cries indignantly.

It's true, I can see the parrot cage and its colorful occupant bobbing away through the crowd.

In 1939, when the war began, I was ten years old and had just started at the girls' school in our county town. The war was a long way off in those days. I only thought about it when the adults gathered around the radio and listened to Hitler's speeches. I tried to listen too, but I understood very little of what he was saying. It always scared me a bit when he shouted like that. Daddy said he had to, or people wouldn't get the message.

Young men being called up—that was something else that reminded us of the war. The railway station was a hive of activity. It was like a big celebration: soldiers proudly wearing their new uniforms and crowds cheering them on their way. They were off to Poland, but everyone was sure they'd be home again in no time.

Wolfgang Kropp from the farm across the way—he had to go too, only a few days after his wedding. His father drove him to the station. I was standing at the garden gate when he said goodbye to his mother, his grandmother and Barbara, his bride. Barbara shed a few tears, but you could tell how proud of Wolfgang they all were.

No, the war wasn't too bad at first. You could still buy enough food, so no one had to go hungry. And all the news was of victories. Everyone talked about our victories. They were delighted to hear how magnificently our soldiers were fighting. I can still hear the fanfares that preceded a special communiqué on the radio. In those days, every special communiqué meant another victory.

There was a big map of Europe hanging up in the lobby at our school. The janitor used to stick lots of little flags in it, moving them forward every day to show how far our soldiers had advanced. Half of Europe belonged to us: Austria, Poland, Czechoslovakia, a big slice of France.

"We're righting an old injustice," I remember Daddy saying. "The territory we're reconquering has always been German and must remain so. Germany must become a great, proud nation once more."

Wolfgang Kropp came home on leave wearing a splendid medal, which we children all admired. He also brought Barbara some French perfume, and she let us sniff it.

But now? Now the enemy are on our soil! The Russians, the French, the British, the Americans—they're closing in on us from all sides. Germany is shrinking fast.

In recent weeks there's been a lot of talk in our village about miracle weapons of some kind—weapons far more effective than the V1 and V2, the unmanned rockets that are fired in Germany and fly all the way to England. So why hasn't Hitler used them yet? We're losing the war, after all! You mustn't say that out loud, though, or you could be in big trouble. In the BDM, the German Girls' League, we were always told: "If anyone doubts that we'll win the war, you must report them, no matter who they are. It's your sacred duty to the nation and our Führer." I heard Granny talking about a hairdresser somewhere in the south of Germany who told a customer: "We lost the war a long time ago." The customer reported her, and she was condemned to death and hanged.

"Clumsy oaf!" a woman behind me mutters. I turn to look. A man in a mustard-yellow storm trooper's uniform, with a peaked cap on his bald head and a bulky suitcase in his hand, is barging through the crowd so inconsiderately that he has almost knocked over a baby carriage. The baby's mother is furious, but she doesn't dare complain too loudly. Any man wearing that mustard-yellow uniform holds a lot of authority. If someone swears at him, he may even get them put in prison. Other people are also staring after him indignantly as he pushes and shoves and jostles his way along, but none of them dares to say what I'm thinking: That lout behaves as if he's a cut above everyone else! What about this "national unity" the authorities keep harping on? Don't they have to obey their own rules?

We came across some rude types like him in the train on the way here. For instance, that fat slob who plunked himself down in an old woman's seat when she had to go to the toilet. When she came back and wanted to sit down again, he simply grinned at her. "No, old girl, your eyes don't deceive you, but I'm also entitled to a seat. I'm sitting here now, and I'm staying put."

Or the woman in the fur coat standing beside the door to the toilet, who swore loudly at anyone who had to squeeze past her to get in there. She kept grousing about the noise the children were making, and the smell, and the luggage stacked in the corridor. "How dare people impose on their fellow passengers like this!" she kept saying. But during the night, when some mugs of hot tea for the grown-ups and warm milk for the children were handed in through the window, she was the first to grab one.

Then there was that family—those three big boys and their grandmother. They really spread themselves out, bringing in more and more of their luggage until it occupied the whole of the middle of the compartment! But they didn't hesitate to demand some chocolate off Erwin and Harald! My brother Erwin is twelve and very sensible. He's quite capable of looking after scatty little Harald.

The big station concourse is absolutely packed. And what a din! People complaining, children crying, shouts and whistles, hurried conversations and, in the background, the occasional hissing and puffing of a locomotive on the move. And us in the midst of it all.

What a draft! The cold is creeping into my bones. It's midwinter—barely halfway through February. I detach my gaze from the irate mother, who's bending over her baby carriage, and peer in the direction Granny went. She's probably in that crowd over there, the long line-up in front of the information desk.

POOR GRANNY. She's sixty-eight, but she's having to take charge of everything now that Mummy isn't with us. In the train coming here she took it in turns to have Rolfi and Harald on her lap. Personally,

I thought Harald was old enough to sit on his own. After all, he goes to school already. I told Granny so, but she whispered: "Even a schoolboy sometimes hankers for a lap to sit on."

You can tell she used to be a schoolteacher, she's so energetic and good at organizing people. There are times when she gets too bossy with Mummy and me and the boys. That annoys me. I'm not a child any longer, after all, and I'm quite capable of making my own decisions. All the same, much as I hate to admit it, what she says is usually right. She's a wonderful woman, really.

Granny has had to take up teaching again. Last year she was called out of retirement, like all the ex-teachers who are still physically fit. That's because so many teachers have been drafted and sent to the front; in fact, quite a few of them have been killed in action. The vacancies have been filled with pensioners. Granny taught second grade until the schools in our district were closed. The class was full to overflowing because of all the young mothers and children who had been evacuated from the cities and sent to the country to escape the bombing.

Life has been getting harder and harder these past four years. Everything is getting scarcer, food most of all. Our allocations of meat, fat and flour, and whatever else was on our ration cards, were steadily reduced. Daddy built us a rabbit hutch and a hen coop while he was home on leave, and Mummy got hold of some young rabbits and hens from somewhere. The eggs and the rabbit meat helped to keep us from going hungry. The Häuslers sometimes gave us beans from their garden, and Mummy gave them cherries and plums from ours. We also swapped things with other neighbors.

Meantime, more and more death notices appeared in the

newspapers. They usually said: "He laid down his life for Führer and Fatherland." More and more parents were informed that their sons had been killed, more and more wives lost their husbands and more and more children their fathers. Wolfgang was killed last year. He won't be coming home again. I still can't believe it, even though his mother showed me the official letter informing her of his death.

Before long, even the older men were called up. Wolfgang's father, for instance, and Daddy. Mummy wept when Daddy left, and so did Granny. He hasn't laid down his life for Führer and Fatherland yet, thank God. Or has he? We aren't at home anymore, we won't be able to receive any mail. We're refugees now, after all.

I glance at the clock. Fifteen minutes past one. Almost half an hour has passed and still no sign of Granny. Rolfi has woken up and is getting restless. If only Granny would come back soon!

2

THE WAR CERTAINLY STOPPED being an uninterrupted series of victory celebrations.

"The Führer has lost his grip," I heard Daddy tell Mummy in a low voice the last time he came home on leave. "He's tried to do too much too quickly."

Oh, Daddy, you and Mummy would never hear a word of criticism against Hitler in the old days. "We Germans have no talent for democracy," I heard you say once. "We need someone to lead us, someone to tell us what's what. Hitler is an ideal leader. He believes in a strong Germany, and he talks sense."

From my earliest childhood I always believed that what you said was right. But do you still think the way you used to now that masses of enemy aircraft have come over and dropped bombs on our cities? Many places are said to be in ruins. The newsreels never show that, but word gets around. Some of my classmates have relations in Hamburg, Berlin and Dortmund, so they know all about the air raids on those cities and tell us terrible stories. Granny said she's sure a lot more civilians have been killed than you ever hear about on the radio.

Then there were the posters. The authorities put them up all over the place, and many of their tattered remains can still be seen. One of them shows a stooping, fog-enshrouded figure in a felt hat with the brim turned down, and beneath it, in bold capitals, are the words:

CAREFUL, THE ENEMY IS LISTENING!

That means you mustn't blurt out anything in public that might be of use to the enemy. Before long, the walls were also plastered with posters depicting the SQUANDER BUG, a sinister black creature with an evil grin and a sack on its back. The Squander Bug harmed the German war effort because it wasted coal, which is rationed and in ever shorter supply. These days there are posters everywhere showing a frightful, fur-hatted Russian with a spiteful grin on his incredibly repulsive face.

The person responsible for all these things is Dr. Goebbels, our propaganda minister, a little man with a limp who looks funny in a peaked cap. The cap is far too big for him, to my mind. Whenever he delivers a speech on a newsreel, he reminds me of a little dog yapping excitedly. The slower the little flags on the maps advanced, the more angrily he barked. Nowadays, when we're making "victorious withdrawals," he gets twice as worked up.

Victorious withdrawals, ha, ha! You can often hear that nonsensical expression on the news, even now, but no one's allowed to laugh at it.

Our neighbors the Häuslers have had a map hanging in their hallway since the beginning of the war. Grandpa Häusler gloated exultantly at first, when we kept winning. I often heard him say: "Our boys are settling old scores!"

I didn't really know what he meant, so I asked Mummy.

She explained that he was talking about our defeat in the First World War.

Grandpa Häusler drew a big circle around our village on the map in red pencil, which made it look like the center of the universe. In the early days of the war, the flags he planted near the red circle moved further and further away, crossing Poland and pushing deep into Russia. But Grandpa Häusler went on sticking the flags in even when they started retreating in the direction of Germany. He is a stickler for honesty, but he ground his teeth when he had to plant a little flag quite close to the red circle. That was only a few days ago.

Rolfi has started crying. He didn't get enough sleep last night. He kept waking up with a start, mainly because of the noise and the icy draft when the doors were opened. And when the train braked sharply. He doesn't understand what's happening these days— he's only a baby, after all. He cried the whole way here, especially when Mummy took him in her arms and kissed him goodbye. He's absolutely bewildered without her—can't understand why she suddenly isn't there anymore. And now Granny has gone too!

Or is he just cold?

He's trying to get off my lap. All right, let him stand up for a bit. He crouches down and reaches for a cigarette end.

"No, Rolfi!" I shove it away with my foot and it disappears into a forest of other people's legs. Rolfi protests. I bend down, pat his cheek and tilt his head back. What a runny nose he's got! I fish a handkerchief out of my overcoat pocket. It's a man's handkerchief—one of Daddy's. Mummy gave me an extra big one before we left, for the little ones' noses. I'm the eldest, after all, so I'm used to looking after them. I wipe Rolfi's nose and pick him up again.

"Granny'll be back in a minute," I tell him consolingly.

"Mummy," he wails. He can already say that word.

I stand up, rocking Rolfi to and fro in my arms, and wiggle my toes inside my shoes to prevent them getting even colder.

Harald is cold too.

"Jump," I tell him. "Jump as high as you can. Keep jumping up and down and flap your arms. You'll be warm soon."

"Why are there so many people in the station?" he asks.

"Because the Russians are getting closer and they're running away from them, like us. This is where they have to change trains; to travel on to friends or relations—or refugee camps. They all want to get away from here as quickly as possible. So do we."

I ought to be glad, really, not having to go to school for a while. I'm in the tenth grade now. My marks aren't bad except in math, but there are times when I dream of playing hooky.

Now I don't have to.

We were simply sent home. That was two weeks ago. The headmaster assembled us in the yard and delivered a short speech. The school would reopen after final victory, he told us. Till then we must grit our teeth and stick it out. He ended by quoting two lines from a song we often sang during break. It came from a film in which the soldiers of Frederick II, the king of Prussia, were hopelessly outnumbered by the enemy and sang it to keep their spirits up. The last two lines went: *Almighty God, ordain that we / be granted final victory.*

"If they're closing the schools," said Grandpa Häusler, "things must be getting really serious."

Granny was growing more and more worried too. "Why aren't we being evacuated?" she kept asking. "Have they forgotten about us?"

Evacuating us meant sending all the civilians to safer places. But it was beginning to seem as if there might not be anywhere safe soon. The radio and the newsreels kept talking about a "counter-offensive" to push the enemy back, but it was launched on the Western Front, not here in the east, and it soon collapsed. "They've run out of steam," was Granny's comment.

Grandpa Häusler said our soldiers were completely exhausted, and no wonder. He still has a piece of shrapnel from the First World War in his knee, which aches when the weather changes. He also has a dent in his forehead. It's deep enough for half a marble to fit into it, but only a little one.

ANOTHER TRAINLOAD OF REFUGEES seems to have arrived. They come pouring out into the concourse, pushing back the people already waiting there. Red Cross volunteers are carrying babies and shepherding old folk along. An elderly man wearing a Red Cross armband calls out "Mothers with babies to the first-class waiting room!" and points down a passage.

Erwin, who's standing beside me, says plaintively: "Do they have to shove like this!"

"Sit on top of our luggage," I tell him, "then they can't bump you. And keep an eye on Harald. Hang onto him. If he struggles, be firm. We'd never find him if he wandered off."

Perched on top of our pile of luggage, both boys look a bit nervous. Even I feel uneasy in the midst of such a crowd, although I'll be sixteen soon.

Very soon, in fact. The day after tomorrow, actually, so we'll celebrate my birthday in Dresden with Mummy's parents. Grandma Glottke is going to bake a cake—she's saved up the ingredients—and Grandpa Glottke has made me a sewing box. He gave that away in his last letter. Perhaps he'll also take me to the theater or the opera for a treat. Oh, no, I'd forgotten: there won't be any more theater or opera till the war's over. Everything's shut. Still, Grandpa is bound to think of something else. Maybe he'll take us all to the movies.

How I'm looking forward to Dresden! It's almost like peacetime there. They do have air-raid warnings, but the enemy bombers just fly over without dropping any bombs, perhaps because even the British and Americans know what a beautiful city it is. I've often heard Grandma Glottke say how glad she is they live in Dresden. "We're safe here," she says.

So we'll get there by tonight, or possibly tomorrow. And the day after that we'll celebrate my birthday, and things won't be so bad because we'll at least have a temporary home with Grandpa and Grandma. At school, whenever one of us has a birthday, the whole class sings a song of her choosing. The teacher wishes her many happy returns and her friends give her little presents. I've missed all that this year. My best friend Elsi Häusler, who lives next door and is in my class, had her birthday three weeks ago. She only just made it.

We had to take a different train from the Häuslers and the Kropps. We got to the station a little later than we should have, and the train meant for people from our village was full to overflowing. The Kropps, who only had two little children with them, squeezed into one compartment and the Häuslers and Elsi got into another, but there wasn't a seat left for Mummy. We had to wait for the next train. That's why Elsi isn't here—no one from our village is.

IT'S GETTING LATE. If only Granny would come back.

I'm sure she never dreamed of having to undergo such an upheaval at her age. There's a picture of a grandmother in Harald's school primer. It shows her sitting in an easy chair, knitting and telling her grandchildren a story. Granny used to do that in the old days. In the last few years any woman who's physically fit has had to help to keep things running while the men are away. Women delivered the mail, drove the buses, served behind counters and even acted as firefighters. Granny's best friend Anna, who lost her husband at about the same time Grandpa Karl, Granny's husband, died, has had to run the big family farm on her own almost since the beginning of the war. Her two sons were called up right away, and both of them have been killed.

Daddy used to do the gardening in the old days. Granny has been doing it since he went away, and the only kind of stories she's told lately have been about the officers who tried to kill Hitler and were condemned to death. Or, only a few days ago, about the big ship with a couple of thousand refugees on board—women, children, old folk and wounded soldiers—which was torpedoed in the Baltic by a Russian submarine and sank immediately. She didn't tell us those awful stories, of course. She told them to Mummy, who made no comment, and only became more and more silent and depressed.

I usually got to know of these stories in any case, because I heard other people talking about them. I could also pick up a lot from the news. After all, I'm not a child anymore.

Soldiers home on leave are another source of inside information. I mean, if anyone knows the truth, they must. Daddy himself said some things on his last leave. I was there when he was about to tell Granny something. He wanted to send me out, but Granny said: "She's fifteen already. Young people grow up faster these days. Let her hear." Then she turned to me. "But keep it to yourself, or your father could get into trouble."

I didn't tell anyone this, but a soldier in his unit was shot by partisans while riding through a forest on his motorbike.

Partisans are enemy guerrilla fighters who try to kill our soldiers. If they're caught, they're hanged. Old Schobert, our history teacher, said this was quite justified: "Cowards who ambush our men instead of fighting fair deserve an ignominious death."

According to Daddy, however, the men who shot his comrade weren't caught. The Russian forests are big and offer plenty of hiding places. But the Germans took it out on the local population to deter the partisans from launching more attacks.

Their revenge was frightful. Five people from the nearest village were arrested at random and hanged: a young woman, two teenage boys and two old men. The people who were hanged probably had nothing at all to do with the partisans.

"The war has taken a terrible turn," Daddy said. "Far worse things are happening—what I've just told you is nothing in comparison."

I've heard the word "terrible" more and more often lately. Three or four days ago I heard Frau Kropp say: "It'll be terrible if we lose the war."

To my mind, things are terrible enough already.

One afternoon before Christmas, when Granny and Mummy were working in the kitchen, I heard Granny say angrily, "How stupid do they think we are? Even a blind man could see we're losing the war!"

"Do you *want* to end up on the gallows?" Mummy snapped at her. Then she caught sight of me standing in the doorway. "Granny was only joking," she said.

I resented that. She was treating me like a child. I know I must keep my mouth shut. I also know that Mummy lost faith in Adolf Hitler several months ago, but she doesn't often show it.

I was a Hitler fan myself until quite recently. At school and in the German Girls' League we were always being told how wonderful he is: how simply he lives and how fond he is of children and dogs. And how bravely he fought in the First World War. And how he never takes any time off, not even an hour lazing in bed on Sundays.

I saw him once in Dresden. Many of the people standing there had tears in their eyes as they waved to him, they were so moved.

Yes, I was wild about Adolf Hitler—or rather, about the Adolf Hitler we saw on the newsreels: a brilliant statesman, a noble character and the father of our nation. I especially remember a sentence from one of his speeches because he laid so much stress on it; in fact, he positively barked it out: "German soldiers are the finest soldiers in the world!" Every newspaper reported it, and our headmaster quoted it in the speech he gave us at the end of the school year. He also told us what the Führer expected German children to be: hard as Krupp steel, tough as leather and swift as greyhounds. But now I wonder whether he wasn't thinking mainly of the boys he needed as soldiers for his war. Since then, even the seventeen-year-olds have been called up.

In the last few weeks I've had a growing suspicion that our Führer is quite a different kind of person, because none of this would have happened if it weren't for the war. If it weren't for the war, I would now be gliding around the village pond on my new ice skates, and we wouldn't be sitting here in this station with a few suitcases, not knowing exactly where Mummy is and how she's doing. And whether Daddy is still alive.

SOMEONE'S CALLING ME. I emerge from my daydream with a start. It's Erwin.

"Twenty minutes to two," he says. "Do you think we'll still get a train to Dresden today?"

I glance at him. He's looking pale and tired. No wonder. He didn't get much sleep last night either.

"Of course we will," I say reassuringly. "Dresden's on the main line."

Erwin sighs. "I can't keep my eyes open."

"Sleep, then," I tell him. "I'll wake you when the time comes."

Erwin stretches out on his stomach on the suitcases. He's asleep almost instantly. Rolfi is quiet now and I think he's nodding off. I have a faint hope that Harald will want to go to sleep too, because he usually copies everything Erwin does, but he's livelier than usual today. There are so many new things to see.

So now I'll have to keep an eye on him as well.

3

I keep thinking of yesterday morning, when Kahlwinkel brought us the news. He'd only just left when old Frau Kropp came hobbling across the road. Everyone calls her "Grula," us included. It means "little grandmother."

"You too?" Grula called over the garden fence.

"Yes, us too," Mummy called back.

"It's out of the question!" Grula shouted. "Our Liese will be calving in the next few days! And what about the hens?"

She was completely beside herself. Grandpa Kropp came and shepherded her back indoors.

Mummy was also in a state, but of a different kind. While Granny went panting up and down the stairs, she stood staring out of the window. We turned on the radio, but the local town wasn't even mentioned, let alone our village. Instead, there were reports that our front line had been "adjusted." That's one of those expressions like "final victory" and "victorious withdrawal"—nothing but a camouflaged lie.

Everything suddenly became hectic. We didn't have a proper lunch, because Mummy said there wasn't time to cook anything.

"Today you can all take anything you like from the larder," she told us.

Even her precious jams and pickles and preserves?

"We'll have to leave it all behind," she said with a sigh.

We needed no second invitation. Like ravening lions, we gorged ourselves on bottled cherries and rhubarb, strawberry, blueberry, and raspberry jam, even quince jelly.

"Don't make yourselves sick," Mummy warned us. All she ate herself was a slice of bread and cheese, and only because Granny talked her into it.

Harald dropped a whole jar of jam, which hit the floor and smashed. Granny went to get a dustpan and brush, but Mummy said: "Why bother? Leave it! We'll be off in a minute."

Her expression conveyed that nothing mattered to her anymore.

"No need for this place to look like a pigsty, even when we're gone," Granny told her. She swept up the broken glass and put it in the dustbin, then mopped the floor.

She eventually persuaded Mummy to help. Lying on the living room table, which we usually ate at, was a big open suitcase. Mummy and Granny fetched things and packed them.

Four heaps of clothes took shape on the sofa. They were the clothes that us children had to wear on the journey—whole mountains of them! Mummy could barely button her coat over her huge tummy, but we had to squeeze into one layer of clothing after another until the seams threatened to burst. Erwin was puffing and blowing and Harald couldn't manage by himself, so I had to help him. He'd eaten and drunk so much he had to keep going to the bathroom.

When he was dressed at last, he wanted his satchel on his back. Although the satchel was his pride and joy, it had to be left behind.

"But I'll be going to school there too!" he protested angrily.

I had to take the satchel out of his hands, and he wept bitterly. Next it was: "My teddy bear, my teddy bear!" I tried to pull it away from him, the grubby, half-bald, dribbled-over creature, but he clung to it and screamed until Granny put her head around the door. "Let him take it," she said. "One teddy won't make much difference."

Then she rejoined Mummy in the living room. The door was ajar, so I could catch what they were saying.

"I'm pretty sure we'll never come back," Mummy said.

"You're always looking on the dark side," Granny told her. "I can well believe the Russians will come through here. They'll wolf the rest of your preserves and trample the flowerbeds. They may even chop up the desk for firewood. But one day we'll come back and restore order."

Maybe, I thought, but would we all be alive by then?

Mummy and Granny kept arguing over what to take and what to leave behind. For instance, Mummy wanted to take her smart straw hat and her high-heeled shoes, which she'd preserved so carefully all through the war. And her grandmother's fine china dinner dishes. What Granny considered important were a pair of thick wool socks and a mug, tin plate and knife, fork and spoon for each of us. Medicines too.

Every now and then Mummy would stop and hold her stomach.

"You go and lie down," Granny told her, and she finished off all the packing with my help. I sat on my bed and cried because I couldn't find Grandpa's hand-carved chess set, the one he gave me shortly before he died. I cursed myself for being so untidy!

At some stage Wolfgang's mother came hurrying across the road.

"What am I to do with Grula?" she wailed. "She refuses to pack anything—she insists on staying put. She dug out the clothes I'd already packed for her, stuffed them under the bedclothes and lay down on top of them. Imagine, she actually hit us! 'Nobody can force me to leave here!' she keeps shouting. 'If the Russians come, let them. If they shell our house I'll be dead, but at least I'll be dead in my own home!' How on Earth are we to get her to go?"

"I'd leave her here," Granny said. "She'll die on you anyway, surrounded by strangers in some place she doesn't know."

"What an indelicate way of putting it!" Mummy said, shaking her head disapprovingly.

"As if delicacy mattered under present circumstances!" Granny retorted.

"*Leave* her here?!" Frau Kropp exclaimed. "All on her own? My husband would never permit it. She *is* his mother, after all!"

And she hurried home again.

The Häuslers from next door were getting ready to leave too. All except for Grandpa Häusler, who had to stay behind "to defend our homeland," as it said on that piece of paper Kahlwinkel brought round. Just when his knee is so painful again, too, from that shell splinter. He limped off to the town hall to inform them of his condition.

He came limping home again before long, shaking his head.

"Know what they told me?" he said. "'You don't pull a trigger with your knee!'"

Grandpa Heckelmayer from two doors down was also forbidden to leave, although there are days when he can scarcely move for his sciatica.

Granny's comment: "I reckon my Karl made himself scarce at the right moment." I missed Grandpa Karl, but maybe Granny was right.

When I hurried one last time through the living room, I saw that the gilded pendulum clock with the dial flanked by two Greek nymphs had disappeared from Daddy's desk. It was said to have come from France and had belonged to my great-great-grandparents. The clock had been handed down from generation to generation and was regarded as a treasured family possession. It surprised me that we were taking it with us. It was valuable, I knew, but awfully heavy. Who was supposed to carry it?

On the way to the station Mummy told me that the clock had been buried, not packed. It was under the mud floor of the cellar. No one would ever suspect it was there.

Harald left his teddy behind on the bed after all, our departure was so rushed. He didn't miss it till we got to the station and wanted to go back for it. He burst into tears, but it was no use.

Harald has fallen asleep too! It's an absolute miracle. He's sitting slumped against our luggage with one knee drawn up. His blue wool hat has slipped sideways. I hope no one trips over him in this crush.

Two o'clock.

Two women in smart coats and hats are squeezing past, grumbling about the chaos and confusion. They aren't carrying suitcases, just handbags, and they aren't wearing several layers of clothes. They can't be refugees—they must live in this town. One of them gives me a nasty look. She's probably wishing the station was like it used to be in peacetime: no trains overflowing with refugees, no dog-tired children sitting on their luggage and waiting, waiting, waiting...

Perhaps soon you'll be sitting on suitcases yourselves, ladies. The war isn't over yet—things could get even worse. They may even get so bad, you won't have a suitcase to sit on. You won't have anything at all, just your lives.

Wolfgang Kropp doesn't even have that.

DADDY, I WONDER IF YOU KNOW that we aren't at home any longer—that our house now stands deserted in the midst of many other dark and deserted houses.

No, you can't possibly know that. You're somewhere at the front with your unit, chilled to the bone and too busy fighting to think of us. That's a good thing, according to Mummy. You wouldn't be able to concentrate on fighting if you knew how much we'd had to leave behind.

Your desk is still at home, Daddy, complete with all its contents except your most important papers and the savings books. And the bookcase and all the books. And your pre-war suits and shoes. Your wedding photo is still on the wall, you know where. All we've taken with us are the photo albums with the pictures of you as a child, and of us. They're somewhere in the luggage. Probably in one of the two suitcases Erwin is asleep on at this moment.

I had to leave my lovely, shiny ice skates hanging on the wall. And the violin Granny got for me in exchange for a quilt. I'd already played it in the school orchestra! When it occurred to me that soon it might be clamped beneath someone else's chin, I had to hold my breath to stop myself from bursting into tears. But last night in the train I'd reached a stage where I felt quite happy at the thought that someone else might play it. Just as long as nobody burns it for the sake of a few minutes' warmth...

Heidi had to stay behind too. I had three dolls as a child, but Heidi was my favorite. It's a long time since I played with her, but she sat on the shelf above my bed and I used to talk to her when I was feeling low. Not out loud, only in my head. She was a comfort. I felt she would always stand by me even if the whole world turned against me. If I'd been younger, I might even have prayed to her. "Please make the war go away," I might have said.

But I'm too old to ask such things of a doll.

We couldn't take dear old Bella with us, either. How she howled when we set off for the station in the Häuslers' farm cart! Erwin and Harald were in tears, and even I couldn't help sobbing then.

"Don't look back," Grandpa Häusler told us. "You'll only make it harder for the poor dog—and yourselves."

He was right. There's no point in looking over your shoulder.

MY HEAD IS ACHING SO BADLY. Should I call out to Granny and hope she'll hear me? She might think something was wrong and come hurrying over for no reason. Then she would have to join the back of the line.

Or should I nip over and try to find her? I'd have to take Rolfi with me. But the boys are all sound asleep. Somebody has to take care of our luggage.

No, it's better to wait where we are.

4

GRANDPA HÄUSLER PROMISED TO FEED BELLA and our rabbits and hens every day. He also promised to look after our house as long as the Russians don't come.

"What if they do?" Erwin asked.

Grandpa Häusler seemed to be debating how to answer that, but Mummy got in first: "They'll be driven back before they get here. Our soldiers will give them such a hiding, they won't feel like trying it again!"

I saw the way Granny glanced at her when she said it. I know that kind of look. It means: "You don't believe that yourself!" But she didn't say anything. On the other hand, she said plenty when Mummy couldn't get a seat at first on the train, although everyone could see she was heavily pregnant. Granny gave the other passengers such a tongue-lashing they eventually moved up and made room for Mummy to sit down. It was a compartment designed for passengers with lots of luggage, fortunately, so at least there was room in the middle for our suitcases. We sat down on them. Granny did too.

A DOG IS SNIFFING our traveling bag. No wonder, it contains the sandwiches and sausages and other "eats," as Granny calls our supplies for the journey. I try to shoo the animal away. It has a smooth, short coat—not black like Bella's, but brown. A woman with a pack on her back is holding the dog on a lead. "Hasso," she calls, "stop that!"

The dog ignores her. It even sniffs Harald. Its warm breath and enquiring nose tickle him awake. He promptly scrambles to his feet and starts patting the animal. Erwin wakes up too, and stares at it fixedly. I suspect we're all thinking the same thing: Hasso was allowed to come, but not our dear, sweet Bella.

Harald resumes hopping up and down once Hasso has gone. He seems to have warmed up—he's even taken off his hat. It's now hanging out of his coat pocket.

"It stinks in here!" he exclaims.

The air reeks of locomotive fumes and cigarette and pipe smoke. Most of the soldiers waiting here for a train are smoking. Standing beside me is one with his right arm in a sling, chain smoking, and enveloping me and the boys in a regular smoke screen.

Daddy smoked like a chimney on his last leave—far more than he used to, and his hands trembled.

How heavy Rolfi is! I glance down at his little round face under its red hat. Luckily, he's still sleeping peacefully.

Thirteen minutes past two.

I stand on tiptoe again and peer across at the information desk.

I can't even see a line-up any longer, just a milling crowd.

"I'm hungry," Erwin sighs.

"Me too," Harald says plaintively.

"We're not eating anything yet," I hear myself say. "Not till Granny's back and we're sitting in the train again."

I'm hungry myself—and how!—but I won't tell the others. A little hunger won't hurt us. If the war gets any worse, food may become even scarcer. Then it'll be a good thing if we've practiced going hungry.

Since the outbreak of war, nearly everything edible has only been available on coupons. I can hardly remember what it's like, living without ration cards. How nice it'll be after the war, when you can go into a shop and buy whatever you like: cakes, roast chickens, grilled sausages! When that day comes, I'll really make a pig of myself.

We've brought our ration cards with us, of course. But...Mummy had them in *her* bag, didn't she? Never mind, Grandpa Glottke will arrange everything. He has some good friends and connections in Dresden. He'll sort it out.

I wonder how Mummy is. She was hoping to make it to Dresden before the baby was born, but our train spent all night stuck between two stations. It was nearly dawn before we got going again, and even then we stopped a few more times. Mummy started moaning. I could see how hard she was trying not to show it, but sometimes she didn't quite succeed. And then, two or three stations down the line—we'd passed Liegnitz by then—she couldn't bear it any longer. The other people in the compartment were growing nervous.

One of them was a woman with a brood of six or seven children.

"If this is her fourth, it could be quick," I heard her say, and an elderly lady muttered, "Surely she isn't going to have it in here, in front of all these children? Where would we get water? She'll have to get out and go to a hospital."

Everyone urged Granny to do something, and Mummy started crying. The next time the train stopped, even before Granny could go and look for the conductor to ask if there was a Red Cross nurse or a midwife on board, several people in our compartment lowered the window and called to the Red Cross volunteers who were dishing out soup on the platform, and they helped Mummy off the train.

It all happened so quickly.

"Don't worry," Granny told her reassuringly. "I'll go on to Dresden with the children and hand them over to your parents. Then I'll come back to get you and the baby. The front line is a long way from here..." And she asked the name and the address of the hospital Mummy was going to be taken to.

Granny was really agitated when we pulled out of the station. Although she knew the name of the hospital and the street it was in, she'd forgotten to ask the name of the town. She consulted the people in our compartment, but nobody knew for sure. The train hadn't stopped right in the station, and I don't remember a sign. All I know is, it must be one or two stations beyond Liegnitz.

Granny meant to ask the conductor when we got out here, but he'd disappeared. As for porters, there didn't seem to be any.

Mummy left the train around ten this morning. It seems ages ago. Now we don't even know where she is. But Granny will go back and find her somehow. Or maybe Mummy will get in touch with Grandpa and Grandma Glottke in Dresden—provided all goes well.

In the town where she is now, things must still be the way they were at home a few weeks ago: everything will still be working, more or less, including the post office. She'd be able to send a telegram.

As long as the Russians don't make a sudden breakthrough. If they captured that town before Mummy...

No, I'd rather not think of it.

My eyelids feel as heavy as lead—they keep drooping—and my feet are like blocks of ice. The minute hand on the clock seems to be moving more and more slowly.

Seventeen minutes past two.

And Granny still isn't back.

I wonder if the baby has been born yet. Is it another little boy? I'd rather it was a girl. Up to now, the boys have outnumbered me three to one.

Rolfi and this latest baby were conceived while Daddy was home on leave. Most of the youngest children in our village are so-called "furlough babies." Mummy wanted four children because it would entitle her to the Mother's Cross. The medal was formally presented to her by the leader of our local German Girls' League. I'd just moved up from the junior branch, and having a mother with a medal made me feel even prouder. Mummy beamed with pleasure, but Granny was far from delighted. She thinks giving a woman a medal for having lots of children turns her into breeding stock—not that she says so too loudly, of course. Most women are pleased to get the medal. Up to now, they say, only men have been awarded medals. At last we've got a chance to win one too.

This latest baby wasn't planned. After the initial shock, though, Mummy was happy about it.

"We'll manage somehow," Granny said. Granny's been a tower of strength to Mummy these last nine months. Mummy gets so depressed, now she's lost faith in Hitler. Granny never thought much of him. She's a born survivor—she went all through the First World War and the hard times that followed it. Daddy once said that Granny is like one of those dolls that always bob up again when you knock them over.

I'm sure Mummy has been thinking a lot about Rolfi, Harald, Erwin and me in the hospital. Before she got out of the train she hugged us all with tears streaming down her cheeks. "Help Grandpa and Grandma as much as you can," she said to Erwin. "Do as Granny and Gisel say and be a good boy," she told Harald. She didn't say anything to Rolfi, just kissed him.

But she looked me in the eye and said, "I'm relying on you."

Granny stayed with Mummy on the platform until they carried her off on a stretcher. The locomotive gave a whistle, and Granny ran back to the train. She managed to reach our carriage at the last moment and scrambled inside when the train was already moving. We were so worried about her, we forgot to wave Mummy goodbye.

And now she's there and the rest of us are here.

5

ALL AT ONCE THERE'S A HORRIBLE, strident wailing sound. It startles everyone and wakes Rolfi. An air-raid warning! That spells danger!

The siren in our local town also went off occasionally—we could hear it from the village. Erwin knows what it means, but not the little ones.

Rolfi is scared and starts crying. Harald clings to my overcoat.

I try to reassure them, but I don't have much time. You have to act fast when an air-raid siren sounds.

Erwin looks at me expectantly. I glance toward the information desk. Granny must come back now, surely! But I can't see her.

Orders blaring from loudspeakers ring out across the concourse: "Everyone proceed to the air-raid shelters! Kindly leave the station at once! You will see signs in the plaza directing you to the air-raid shelters!"

Jostled from behind by new arrivals, people are already on the move. They stream toward the exit, in our direction. We're in their path. Shouts, plaintive cries, children bawling. Erwin hurls himself on top of our luggage and spreads his arms and legs in an attempt to protect it.

But we're being pushed along. I hug Rolfi to me with one arm and grab our bag of food with my right hand.

"Hang on tight!" I tell Harald, who has started crying. "Stay with me!" He clings to my overcoat pocket.

An elderly woman is shoved in the back and falls on top of Erwin.

"We've got to get out of here!" I call to him. "We've got to go with the others!"

"What about the luggage?" I hear him ask in a muffled voice.

Yes, the luggage. Mummy took the suitcase containing her clothes and the baby things when she got off the train, but there are two more suitcases standing there: a big one with our clothes and shoes and a smaller one containing Granny's things. And Granny's backpack with the blankets in it.

Erwin can't possibly carry all those. I'm still debating what we need most—apart from the food—when I'm swept away by the crowd.

"Erwin!" I yell. "Leave it all and come with us!"

I turn to look for him and almost get knocked over. Where is he?

Rolfi and Harald are both crying harder now.

"Erwin!" I shout. "Where are you?"

No reply.

I've no choice but to hurry along with the rest. If I tried to turn back, they would trample me underfoot. They're in a panic, that's why. Railway stations are favorite targets during air raids, everyone knows that—even I do. I heard Grandpa Häusler and Granny talking about it.

"I've got to pee!" Harald wails at my side.

"Wait," I tell him. "We'll be outside soon…"

Frantically, I wonder how to find Erwin. I keep looking over my shoulder and calling his name as loud as I can. I shout for Granny too. I can see the exit ahead. We're getting nearer and nearer. I decide to let the human tide wash me through the exit with Rolfi and Harald. Then we'll hug the wall and wait for Erwin. He's bound to come out here—or are there some side exits? I feel like crying. What if I lose him? Mummy's relying on me, after all!

Beside me, a child falls over—a girl of seven or eight. Her mother hauls her to her feet. A moment later a fat, elderly woman falls over too. She can't get up. People step over her, cursing. "Please help me up!" I hear her call in a panic.

Harald tugs at my overcoat pocket.

"Don't pull like that!" I snap at him.

"But I almost let go, they're pushing and shoving so hard," he wails. "And I need to go so badly."

"Outside," I tell him breathlessly. "Outside!"

I feel a sudden, violent tug at my coat. Then I hear a cry: "Gisel!"

Harald's voice. Startled, I turn to look. He should be holding on to my pocket! Why has he let go? I feel a mixture of shock and anger. Why can't he at least do as he's told in a desperate situation like this?

"Where are you?" I call anxiously. He's only six. A little shrimp like him in a crush like this!

Then, looking indignant and reproachful, he squeezes between two soldiers, waving a rectangular piece of cloth: my pocket.

Thank God, I've got him back. My knees have gone all limp with shock. I'd like nothing better than to pick him up and give him a hug. But I'm holding Rolfi in one arm and carrying the food bag with my other hand. I don't dare put them down.

"Hang onto the bag," I tell Harald gently. "Really, really tight. Hold it by the handle—that won't come off."

"If we don't get outside soon," I hear him say, "I'll do it in my pants."

Go ahead, then, I think. We've lost Erwin. Nothing matters compared to that.

AS WE EMERGE FROM THE STATION, I take shelter against the wall on the right. There's a big mound of cleared snow there. Harald and I climb on top of it and I put the bag down. Now we're above the crowd. Rolfi has put his arms round my neck and is nuzzling my cheek. His cheeks are wet with tears.

My arm, my arm! It's aching like mad. Rolfi is so heavy, but I can't put him down, it would be too dangerous. He might slither down the heap of snow and get trampled in the crush.

"You can have a pee now," I tell Harald hurriedly. "But do it against the wall, and try not to splash your shoes."

I quickly survey the station plaza while he's relieving himself.

The thin layer of snow is mottled by innumerable footprints. An occasional snowflake comes drifting down. Groups of people are streaming in different directions.

"Where's Erwin?" Harald asks.

At that moment I hear Erwin calling from inside the concourse: "Gisel! Gisel!"

It's like an electric shock. His voice came from near the exit, so he should come out here. We mustn't miss him or we'll never find each other again!

"Erwin!" I call back. "Yes, here I am! Outside, here!"

I quickly shove the bag against the wall with my foot.

"But it's wet there!" Harald calls reproachfully, still fiddling with his fly buttons.

"That doesn't matter now," I tell him hurriedly. "Listen, you stay here with the bag and look after it. Don't let it out of your sight! Our food's in there. If we lose the bag, we won't have anything to eat. Stay up here on this heap of snow, right against the wall, or you'll get lost in the crowd. I'll be right back—I'm just going to get Erwin."

Holding Rolfi in my right arm, because my left arm has gone numb, I climb down off the mound of snow and thread my way back to the exit. A quick glance over my shoulder reassures me that Harald is standing against the wall with the bag beside him. He's just pulling his blue hat on, and his eyes are fixed on the bag. Good boy!

Now for Erwin. He's bound to find me if I keep calling his name.

"Erwin!" I call. "Erwin! Erwin!"

I catch a glimpse of his face among the people pouring out of the station. Then it disappears again. The big clock in the concourse says it's twenty-four minutes past two. Has it stopped? Only three minutes since the siren sounded?

"Faster, faster!" I hear a policeman call somewhere behind me. "Keep moving!"

"Erwin!" I shout, plunging into the crowd.

"Hey, you!" calls a woman with an armband. She tugs at my sleeve. "The shelter is over there!"

She points back the way I've come, the direction in which most of the crowd is hurrying: across the plaza and to the right. I couldn't care less about the air-raid shelter, not right now, so I shake her hand off. Erwin is my sole concern. There he is again! He stretches out his arm and I manage to grab it. I haul him out of the crowd and put my free arm around him.

"I only managed to save the backpack," he gasps, looking guilty. "I tried to drag the suitcase with our things along, but there was such a crush I had to let go of it."

"It doesn't matter," I tell him breathlessly. "We're together again, that's the main thing."

"Where's Harald?"

"He's guarding the food bag."

But when I turn and point to the heap of snow, there's no sign of Harald or the bag. All I can see is a Red Cross woman bending over, pulling up her stockings.

"But he was there a moment ago," I say, appalled.

Erwin runs up to the woman. "Excuse me, have you seen a little boy with a big bag?" He indicates Harald's approximate height by holding up his hand. "He's six. His name is Harald."

The woman shakes her head.

"He was here a minute ago," I add, my heart pounding.

"Someone must have taken him off to a shelter," the woman replies, straightening up.

I climb onto the mound of snow and quickly scan the plaza. It's a big square with several streets running off it. People are scuttling this way and that through the falling snow and disappearing down the side streets. Policemen are shouting and gesticulating as they try to steer them in the right direction.

"Harald wouldn't go anywhere with a stranger," I hear myself say.

"Then someone must have picked him up and carried him," the woman snaps, losing patience. "It's wrong to leave a little boy like that on his own, especially in an air raid."

"But the bag has gone too," I say, close to tears. "Besides, he'd have called me. I wasn't far away."

"The three of you should get to a shelter too, and fast, if you value your lives," the Red Cross woman insists. "No bombs have fallen yet, but that doesn't mean—"

"Where is it, the shelter?" Erwin breaks in. "We're strangers here."

"There's a big one there"—she points to the right—"and some smaller ones over there." She points in the opposite direction. "The big one is nearest. Just follow those people—they're making for it. You're bound to find your little brother when the all-clear goes."

"He must be in one of the shelters," I say to Erwin.

He nods. "In the big one, probably."

Quick, down from the mound of snow and to the right. We must hurry. We don't want to be caught in the open if the bombers come and really drop bombs. I climb down carefully. Fall with Rolfi in my arms? It doesn't bear thinking of!

Erwin promptly loses his footing. He slides down the snow on his bottom, right into the midst of the hurrying crowd. Someone trips over him and swears. He gets back on his feet and apologizes. He's lucky—the backpack saved him from bruising his backside. It must hurt, but only a little, because he's wearing three pairs of trousers and two pairs of underpants. It's less of an effort to wear something than carry it, Mummy said. Me, I'm wearing three sets of underwear and two skirts and a dress over my tracksuit bottoms.

"That's right," Granny told us. "At least you won't be cold, wrapped up like that, even if the worst happens…" What would Granny say now, I wonder? I wish she were here to tell us what to do.

We stumble off, the fresh snow crunching beneath our feet. I'm carrying Rolfi; Erwin has the backpack. A snowflake in my eyelashes melts and trickles into my eye.

"Hurry!" a policeman calls to us. "The bombers could be here any moment!"

People are running, struggling with their heavy luggage, children are crying. A suitcase has burst open and is lying in the snow with clothes spilling out of it: a brassiere, a lady's shoe. A woman bends over it, another woman drags her away. We're being jostled and buffeted by the tide of humanity. Stay on your feet, I tell myself. Don't fall over whatever you do!

I see people pouring out of the station by a side entrance. Could Granny have come out there instead of the main exit? If so, she must be in the shelter we're headed for.

But finding Harald is more important. Granny can look after herself.

Just before we reach the air-raid shelter we're met by a mass of agitated people hurrying in the opposite direction. "It's no use!" they gasp. "They aren't letting anyone else in."

We press on regardless. A man wearing an armband, an air-raid warden, waves us away.

"Get to the other shelter, quick!" he barks at us. "This one's full to overflowing. I've already let in far more people than I should."

"We only want to see if our little brother is inside," I tell him in despair.

"Come back after the all-clear!" he shouts hoarsely.

Then he slams the door in my face. I hammer on it with my fist.

"Stop it," Erwin says. "There's no point."

We turn and hurry back across the plaza. It occurs to me that, wherever Harald has got to, he can't be carrying that heavy bag. It's gone, come what may. We've lost all our food.

I'm exhausted, and Rolfi is slipping from my grasp. Panting hard, I stop and set him down in the snow. He starts crying.

"Shall I carry him?" Erwin gasps. "If you take the pack, I'll give him a piggyback."

A piggyback—that's a good idea, but I'll take him on my back. If we got separated again for any reason, Rolfi would be too much for Erwin to cope with on his own and I'd have an awfully bad conscience. I quickly get Erwin to hoist him onto my back.

Rolfi knows about piggybacks. He promptly winds his arms around my neck and lifts his little legs so I can clamp them to my sides. Now I can walk faster. Erwin is a good way ahead. The pack is so bulky, I can't see his head from behind.

"Faster, faster," he calls. "I think I can hear the bombers!"

I glance at the station entrance. The last time I saw Harald, he was standing on the mound of snow beside it.

There's a big round clock above the canopy. It's twenty-nine past two. Only five minutes since we were standing on that mound of snow!

People are still pouring out of the station, many carrying heavy bags, and most of them women and children. A group of elderly people is being shepherded along by three nuns. They're making for the air-raid shelters, but very slowly. Will they get there in time? I'm sorry for the old folk. They're being overtaken by younger people.

Could Granny be leaving the station only now?

She would have spotted us, though. She's got good eyesight in spite of her age, the plaza is fairly empty now. She would surely have called to us.

It's a mercy she isn't here at this moment, because she'd ask where Harald is. We simply must find him before *she* finds *us*.

We may never see him again, and it'll be all my fault. I sob despite myself. I hope Erwin doesn't hear...

Through my tears I dimly see that we've now reached the mouth of a side street. Half blinded, I bump into Erwin, who's been waiting for me. I wipe my eyes on my sleeve. There's a sign on the wall pointing downward:

PUBLIC AIR-RAID SHELTER

But a policeman is standing guard outside, a regular man mountain with a big mustache. "There's no room!" he yells hoarsely. "We weren't prepared for such a horde of refugees. Cross the street and take the turn four doors farther along. It's the second building on your left! You'll find another shelter there!"

A couple supporting an old man plead with him. "Please let us in. Surely you can—"

"No, damn it!" he bellows. "They're packed like sardines already!"

"But our little brother's in there!" I cry, pushing forward. "We've got to join him!"

"He'll be safe in the shelter," the policeman growls. "It can wait till the all-clear goes!"

An old woman's suitcase slips through her fingers. The policeman goes to help her. As he bends down, a cry of pain escapes his lips and he clasps his back. No wonder. He's as old as she is.

The people in front of us hurry across the deserted street and turn. Between the second and third buildings on the left, which are at least five stories high, is an alley leading to a door with another shelter sign. We dash toward it. The air-raid warden stationed there, a man wearing an armband and a steel helmet, waves us away. We beg and plead until he eventually lets us in. A steep flight of stairs leads downward.

I don't know how he's managed it but, in the middle of all this noise and chaos, Rolfi has fallen asleep. I cradle him in my arms.

"They're coming!" we hear the air-raid warden bellow from behind us.

The muffled drone of aircraft engines grows louder. Erwin and

I know that droning sound. Planes sometimes fly over our village—our own planes, and the enemy's. I can even remember hearing the drone of engines before the war. It sounded just the same. *If only I could fly!* I used to think whenever I heard it.

The air-raid warden pushes us roughly into the cellar from behind. A metal door slams, and a heavy bolt squeaks into place.

6

I CAN'T HEAR THE ENGINES ANYMORE, probably because the door is shut. Or possibly because there's so much noise in here, mainly children crying. Or because the enemy planes have already been and gone.

"They might as well sound the all-clear," says someone behind me. "The danger is over. They never drop any bombs on this place and they follow a different route on the return trip. It's always been like that."

The shelter can't be more than twice the size of our school classroom. The ceiling isn't level, though; it's vaulted and supported by columns. It reminds me of a crypt like the one Grandpa Glottke showed me in Dresden once.

Some people are sitting, trying to get comfortable; others are standing jammed together in front of the door to the outside world. "If the train is late," somebody says, "we'll still catch it." And a little later, impatiently: "Why don't they sound the all-clear, damn it? Those planes must be long gone by now!"

Summoning up all my strength, I shout, "Harald!" Erwin shouts for him too.

Then we hold our breath and listen, hoping to hear him above the din.

And again: "Harald!"

Harald knows my voice, and his own is so loud and high-pitched, he could make himself heard if he wanted to.

But there's no response, no delighted cry of "Gisel!" So he doesn't appear to be here.

"Perhaps he's asleep," Erwin says in my ear. "You know what he's like when he's tired, he sleeps like a dormouse."

He removes the backpack and sits on it. I can tell how tired he is. I'm completely exhausted. As for Rolfi, even my shouting didn't wake him.

Erwin asks me something, but I can't make it out; there's too much noise in here. He has to shout. "Want me to take Rolfi for a bit?"

Oh, Erwin! I almost say yes, it would be so nice to get rid of my burden. But then I picture what would happen if panic broke out—if everyone made a sudden dash for the exit, for instance. With Rolfi on his lap, Erwin wouldn't stand a chance.

How stuffy it is! The air reeks of sweat and tobacco smoke. I look around. There's no daylight down here, just a few dim electric bulbs dangling from the ceiling. There isn't even enough light to read by.

As my eyes get used to the gloom I can see that the cellar is chock-full. People are standing jammed together or sitting on their luggage. Now and then I catch a brief glimpse of benches running around the walls, filled with the lucky ones who managed to get a seat. The air-raid warden must have seen to it that a certain amount of discipline prevailed, because nearly all of them are mothers with little children or old folk or wounded soldiers—or people who are obviously sick. Most of the men are standing. The soldiers were probably in transit and had to change trains here. Then the air-raid warning caught them.

This isn't my first experience of an air-raid shelter. We went to the school cellar in our town several times, usually during class. Once, when we were supposed to be doing a math exam, we welcomed the interruption. We sat there in the school cellar, horsing around in the silliest way because we could be pretty sure the enemy bombers were only passing over. Their usual targets were towns in Austria. But I also had to go to the public air-raid shelter a few times in the afternoon, and twice in Dresden, so I know what to expect.

"We need to find ourselves a place near the wall," I tell Erwin. "Otherwise we could get knocked over when they open the door again. But not too far from the exit. If Harald is here, we want to make sure he doesn't slip out when the all-clear sounds."

We proceed to squeeze between the grown-ups.

"Stay put, damn you!" a soldier snaps at us.

"We need the toilet," Erwin tells him.

He hurriedly makes way for us.

"Good thinking," I whisper in Erwin's ear. It hadn't occurred to me, but it's true. I need to go too. It's just that I didn't have time to think of it before.

On the left, near the exit, is a wooden bench full of old people and mothers with little children. Beside it stands a table at which two women are busy changing their babies' diapers. I think about changing Rolfi, but I don't want him to wake up and make a fuss.

I bend down and look beneath the table. There are some stacks of cardboard boxes under there, but they could be shoved back a bit to make room for Erwin. I point this out to him, and he stoops and pushes the boxes aside.

"What are you up to?" one of the women asks sharply.

She peers down at us. Erwin has pushed the backpack into a gap and is sitting in front of it with his knees drawn up.

"Oh, all right," she says, and takes no more notice of him. Her baby is screaming like a stuck pig.

"Would you like to sit here with Rolfi?" he calls up to me. "Then I could go and look for Harald."

I shake my head. "No, I'll go. You stay here and get some sleep. If we get separated for any reason, we can meet at that heap of snow in front of the station—where we were before."

Erwin nods and says something. He has to repeat it before I understand: "And if we don't find each other there, I'll make my way to Dresden. I know the address, after all."

Yes, Mummy made Erwin and Harald learn Grandpa and Grandma Glottke's address by heart—they could say it in their sleep. That's some comfort, at least. For safety's sake, though, Harald is also wearing a label under his sweater with his name and the Dresden address on it. He can't read what it says, but he could show it to a grown-up and ask for help. Rolfi is wearing a label like that too. Mummy thought of all "eventualities," as Granny calls them.

Rolfi is stirring against my shoulder, probably woken by my voice. I hold him tight and bend down. Now Erwin can understand me even if I whisper.

"I'm going to make a tour of the cellar," I tell him. "It may take a while."

He nods. His eyelids are already drooping.

I START TO SQUEEZE THROUGH THE CROWD. There are mountains of luggage everywhere, and it's a job to get past. I keep looking for a blue hat. Is Harald still wearing it, or is it back in his pocket? The light is so dim, I can scarcely tell one color from another.

It's so warm. And so stuffy! Smoking is forbidden down here, but the soldiers' uniforms are saturated with tobacco smoke. Daddy was like that when he came home on leave, reeking of tobacco smoke and sweat. The smell simply wouldn't go away.

Daddy didn't smoke half as much before the war as he has since joining the army—or rather, since he's been at the front. He's just like his comrades: they smoke before going into action, to soothe their nerves when they're lying on the bare ground with the enemy shell bursts coming nearer and nearer, and they know that some of them will be hit. Daddy doesn't talk about it much, certainly not to us, but he did let slip that he prays—"Please God, let me make it!"—and that he sweats with fear. He's even done it in his pants before now—him, a grown-up man! But I don't think less of Daddy for that. I don't turn up my nose in disgust when a soldier smells of tobacco smoke and sweat.

Poor Daddy, the last time I saw him he'd developed two furrows in his forehead that weren't there before, and bags beneath his eyes. And his expression was so different—far harder than before he was sent to the front. He looked angry, somehow. He never mentioned Hitler anymore, and he quarreled with Mummy more often, though always behind closed doors. Even Harald noticed how different he'd become.

I must concentrate on Harald or I'll miss him, so I look out for young children. My progress is slow because I have to peer in all directions. I see sleeping children everywhere: among the luggage, on the floor, on women's laps. Sometimes, when they're muffled up in blankets, I can't tell how old they are.

"Looking for someone?" an old woman asks me.

"My little brother," I tell her. "Six years old, brown curly hair, blue wool hat. We lost him when the air-raid warning went."

She casts a sympathetic glance at Rolfi's sleeping form. "So there are three of you?" she asks.

I shake my head. "No, four. Erwin's over there. He's twelve."

"Where's your mother?"

"She isn't here. She's having a baby."

The old woman shakes her head. "What times these are!" She feels in her bag and brings out a handful of cookies.

"Left over from Christmas," she says. "I hope you enjoy them."

What a wonderful gift! I thank her delightedly, but I don't eat any of the cookies. I stow them in my remaining overcoat pocket. We'll have to make do with them, now that we've lost our bag of food. Erwin and Rolfi must be very hungry, and Harald will have his share when we find him.

I'm hungry myself, of course. Very hungry, in fact, but I can grin and bear it. I'm responsible for the others for as long as Granny isn't with us.

But I need the toilet quite badly. Is there one down here? Of course, there's a toilet in every public air-raid shelter, but where?

The air-raid warden, who has a little toothbrush mustache like Hitler's, has climbed on a chair in the middle of the cellar. He has removed his helmet and is holding a sort of speaking trumpet to his lips to amplify his voice. Without it, he probably wouldn't be able to make himself heard above the hubbub.

"Attention, attention!" he calls. "Listen, please, I've an important announcement to make!"

The noise dies down. Everyone wants to hear the latest. Only the very youngest children go on squawling.

"I've got three lost children here," the man calls. "Will their parents or anyone who knows anything about their parents kindly report to me at once!"

I almost drop Rolfi, I'm so overjoyed. One of the three must be Harald! I start threading my way over to the man on the chair.

He lowers the trumpet. A child is handed up to him—a baby no more than a year old. It utters a series of piercing screams as he lifts it up and turns on the spot, holding it under the arms. I hear a woman's voice ring out from the other end of the cellar—"Franzi! Franzi—at last!"—and catch a glimpse of her. She, too, has trouble forging a path through the crowd, but she eventually takes possession of her baby. Laughing and weeping simultaneously, she hugs and kisses it.

"My God, how worried she must have been," a woman near me sighs. "A child can so easily get lost in a crush like this..."

It's lucky Mummy doesn't know that Harald has disappeared. How worried *she* would be!

I crane my neck. Who's next?

The air-raid warden picks up another child. This one is much older, maybe six or seven. A girl dressed up like a doll. Her hood is lined with real fur, all white and fluffy, and she's wearing red boots and little gold earrings. Her face is tear-stained.

"This is Lotte!" the man calls, turning on the spot with her. "Lotte Scheider, seven years old, from Festenburg. She got separated from her mother in the station. Is her mother here?"

"Mummy!" the girl sobs. Then, suddenly, in a pathetic voice: "Marta!"

No response. Nobody puts a hand up.

"No relations or neighbors here?" the man calls. "No one called Marta?"

Still no response. He puts Lotte down again. I see him whisper something to her, probably something comforting. I feel sorry for her, of course, but I'm already elbowing my way closer to the man, intent on seeing the next child. It's *got* to be Harald!

But it isn't. A girl of around three is handed up and displayed to everyone. Her name is Hannelore, and her hair is braided into tiny pigtails. Not wanting to be held in the air, she kicks and struggles. I've almost reached the man on the chair by now, so I'm near enough to hear the girl's grandmother say she lost sight of her in the station and is relieved to see her again. The person still missing is Hannelore's mother, who left her with her grandmother, saying she needed to go to the toilet, and hasn't been seen since. The old woman asks the air-raid warden to call her daughter.

"Does anyone know anything about Hannelore's mother, Gerda Witten from Strehlen?" the man bellows into his speaking trumpet.

No answer.

Somebody behind me says: "What's the betting she seized the opportunity to dump the child and clear off?"

A man's hoarse voice growls: "Plenty of people find all this chaos very convenient."

Hannelore is returned to her grandmother, a bent-backed old woman who walks with a cane. The child is a lively little thing and wants to run around. The old woman is in despair. A Red Cross volunteer picks the girl up and takes the grandmother's arm.

"My God," I hear the first voice say with a sigh, "just look: that child is far too much of a handful for the old lady. If they catch the mother, they should punish her severely!"

I'm right beside the chair now. The air-raid warden climbs down.

"Haven't you found another child?" I ask him hurriedly. "A boy of six? My brother Harald?"

He shakes his head. "Perhaps he's in another air-raid shelter."

Yes, perhaps, but perhaps not. Perhaps he's looking for us somewhere outside in the plaza, or in the station itself. He must be freezing cold...

I give up in despair and make my way back to Erwin. If only I knew where the ladies' room is!

Then I see the girl named Lotte beside me. She's all by herself, staring into space with tear-stained cheeks and her arms dangling limply at her sides. Erwin and Rolfi have me, at least, but Lotte is all alone the way Harald must be now. No one to look after her, no one to comfort her. She's seven years old. In her first year at school, or maybe her second.

I feel so sorry for her. Cautiously, I slip my hand into hers. She gives a start and looks up at me with a delighted smile, but her face promptly falls and she starts to cry. Her nose is running, and I take out my handkerchief. It's in my overcoat pocket with the cookies. I must be careful not to drop any, or I'd have to bend down and pick them up. It would be too hard with Rolfi in my arms. Besides, someone might step on them. Now that we've lost the bag, they're precious.

I wipe Lotte's nose and pocket the handkerchief again.

"I thought you were Marta," she sobs. She's wearing a red ribbon in her long, smooth, dark hair.

"Who's Marta?" I ask. "Your sister?"

She shakes her head. "My nanny. She's a bit taller than you. Fatter, too, but her hand feels almost like yours."

Oh yes, I put my hand in hers.

"But Marta didn't come in the same train as us," she sighs. "She went with her mother and her brothers and sisters. Mummy and I traveled on our own. She was so angry, she kept saying: Don't ask so many questions, stop crying, stop whining. She even tweaked my ear! She's never like that at home. I'd rather have gone with Marta, she's much nicer to me."

Lotte sniffs.

"How did you get separated from your Mummy?" I ask.

"She was holding my hand," Lotte says with a sigh, "and walking awfully fast—dragging me behind her. When I couldn't keep up she scolded me and tugged at my arm. But then, when the siren went off, people started running and pushing so hard, she let go of me. I couldn't find her again."

So that's how it was. I draw a deep breath. Mummy would never have treated us like that, nor would Granny. Nor would Grandpa and Grandma Glottke.

"And then?" I say. "How did you end up in here?"

"I was all alone in that big square. I was crying because I didn't know what to do, so that man took me with him and brought me here."

"The one who lifted you up just now?"

Lotte nods.

Uneasily, I reflect that Harald may have been in the same position.

What will the air-raid warden do with Lotte when the all-clear goes? He has so many people to look after down here, he'll probably hand her over to the Red Cross people.

7

I WANT TO HELP LOTTE, but I have to keep going. I have to find Harald. Then I remember the cookies. I surreptitiously count them. Seven. Enough to give Lotte one and leave two each for my brothers.

I give Lotte a cookie. She beams at me and wolfs it down in no time. I get ready to move on "Well, bye-bye, I hope you find your Mummy and Marta very soon."

But then, with a sob, she seizes my hand and clings to it.

"Don't go!" she pleads, tugging at my hand.

"But the man will look after you," I say.

She bursts into tears. I can hardly understand her, but I finally make out what she's trying to say: "He'll be angry with me for crying!"

"But I can't stay with you," I tell her sadly. "Erwin's waiting for me over there. That's one of my brothers, and I'm looking for another."

"I'll come with you then," she says through sobs.

What am I to do? I can't leave her crying like this. Where's the air-raid warden? I can't see him anywhere, just the chair with the speaking trumpet lying on it. If I take Lotte with me, I must let him know that I'll look after her while we're here in the cellar, but I can't go looking for him *as well!*

The first thing I need to do is get back to Erwin, then I can give him Rolfi to hold while I go to the toilet. I can tell the man later. I'll hand Lotte back to him as soon as people start leaving the shelter when the all-clear goes.

I've no need to tow Lotte along because she's clinging to my coat.

"What should I call you?" she asks.

Will she feel surer of me if she knows my name, or does she want to be able to call me if we get separated?

"Gisela," I tell her. "At home everyone calls me Gisel."

I keep looking around for blue hats, checking children's faces and calling Harald's name. The shelter isn't *that* big. He ought to hear me.

Unless he's asleep.

Lotte continues to cling to my coat. I don't let her take hold of my remaining pocket. That I need for my handkerchief—and the cookies.

Another woman, this time a young Red Cross nurse, asks if I'm looking for someone. I tell her about Harald.

"I thought you might be looking for your mother," she says, glancing at Lotte and Rolfi, who's still asleep. "Where is she?"

I think quickly. I'm not an adult yet. If she discovers I'm only fifteen—well, nearly sixteen—and that I'm having to look after my brothers on my own, she may take us with her and put us in some Red Cross hostel where Granny will never find us. Or in a children's home.

"She's looking for Harald too," I say quickly, but I avoid her eye and stare past her. I don't like lying.

Someone calls to the nurse to attend to an old woman who's stretched out on the bench behind us, gasping for breath. We're rid of her.

Before I can move away with Lotte, a fat woman sitting on a little folding chair plucks at my sleeve. She has a hat perched at an angle on her permed hair and a fox fur around her neck, complete with head, legs and tail. The fox's jaws are biting its tail. A teacher at our school wears a fox fur like that—used to wear one, I mean. We only had her for music, luckily. I never liked her, that's partly why I don't care for fox furs—and why I don't take to this fat woman, either. Why would she tug at my sleeve?

I shake off her hand and start to push through the crowd. Then I hear her call after me: "Was your Harald wearing a blue hat?"

My nerves give a jolt. I stop short and swing round.

"Yes," I say. "Have you seen him?"

She shrugs. "No idea if it really was your brother, but it could have been, judging by his age. He was wearing a big blue wool hat and following a man who was carrying a bag. The man was walking so fast the boy found it hard to keep up. At one point the boy slipped in the snow and fell down. The man glanced over his shoulder a couple of times but didn't stop. But the boy gradually caught up to him. He kept shouting: "That's our bag!"

"Yes," I exclaim happily, "that was him! Where did you see him?"

"On the way to this shelter," the woman replies.

So he must be here. Great news! I feel like throwing my arms around her, but I can't with Rolfi in my arms, so I can only say thank you. Reluctantly, I decide to part with another cookie, but she only smiles and shakes her head. Her fox's beady glass eyes glitter at me.

"I've got plenty of food with me," she says, pointing to a big bag lying beside her chair.

Perhaps she'll give me some, I think, but she makes no move to do so. Should I ask her? I don't have the nerve.

Now to get back to Erwin and tell him the wonderful news: Harald is somewhere in here!

And then I must go to the toilet.

I'm shoved and jostled and get my feet stepped on. Rolfi wakes up because his hat has slipped over his face. He's snuffling. I'm sure he's dribbled on my collar and my scarf.

"Damnation, what's the matter with them?" I hear a man complain. "The all-clear should have sounded long ago. Doesn't anything work here anymore? We've been stuck in this lousy, stuffy hole for over half an hour!"

Only half an hour? It seems as if we've been here for an eternity.

Standing beside the exit is the air-raid warden, the man who stood on the chair and called out the children's names. I hear men and women talking together excitedly.

"Open the door! We've got to get back to the station!"

"Be reasonable, the all-clear hasn't gone yet!"

"But the bombers must be—"

"They should have sounded the all-clear ages ago. The siren must have failed!"

"At least let us take a look outside!"

"It's on your own head then!"

The man certainly won't have the time to listen about Lotte. I don't have the time, either. With Lotte in tow, I push past the people arguing with him. The door creaks open, light streams in, cold air fans my legs. The cellar is filled with agitated voices:

"The door's open! Anyone who wants to leave, can!"

"Stay here, stay here, the all-clear hasn't gone yet!"

"So what? They're only flying over us on their way to somewhere else!"

Lotte is looking thoroughly disheveled by the time we reach the changing table. Erwin is still beneath it, thank goodness. He's asleep sitting up with his head on his knees. I give him a gentle shake and tell him what I've heard. The news jolts him awake. He looks puzzled.

"So why haven't you found him?" he asks.

Yes, why haven't I? I think for a moment. Then it occurs to me that my tour of the cellar ended at the air-raid warden's chair. Harald must be over on the other side!

"Now I'll look," Erwin says, crawling out from under the table. "You can have a rest, but don't forget to draw your knees up, or you'll get stepped on by people on their way to the toilet. It's just over there, I've been there myself. Ladies' on the left, men's on the right. I left the pack under the table so no one would take my place, but I was so scared it would be stolen, I almost couldn't pee."

He points to the left.

"You wait here for me," I say quickly, thrusting Rolfi into his arms. It's such a relief not to have to carry him any longer. I arch my back and stretch my arms, accidentally nudging an old woman.

"Do you mind?" she snaps.

Lotte tugs at my sleeve. "I need to go too. Now."

"Who's that?" Erwin asks.

"Lotte," I say, and I give him a brief explanation of why she's with me.

I open my overcoat pocket and let him peek inside.

"Six of them," I tell him with pride. "You see? We won't starve, even without our food bag."

"Six cookies won't go far," he says drily. "There are five of us now, counting her and Harald."

"Still, they're better than nothing at all."

"When the all-clear sounds," he says, "let's go back to the station. There was a great big container of soup on the platform, for the refugees."

I remember seeing it. The soup was steaming hot, but Granny didn't want to waste any time getting to Dresden, so she steered us past it. After all, we had our own food at that point.

"I need to go now, Gisel," demands Lotte. She's still holding on to my sleeve.

I heave a sigh.

"I'm sure they'll let us have some soup," Erwin says, "even if we did get off the train this morning."

Then I remember that the door is open. I peer across the cellar. The mob of people wanting to leave is growing steadily bigger.

What if Harald takes it into his head to leave too, perhaps because he thinks we're among that crowd?

Erwin notices the people pouring out of the shelter.

"Has the all-clear gone?" he asks, looking puzzled.

I shake my head. "But what if Harald...?"

Erwin comes up with a solution. "Until you get back from the toilet, I'll stand beside the exit and see if he appears."

"In that bunch? You might not see him at all, and you can't fight your way through the crowd with Rolfi in your arms." At this moment Rolfi, who has been sniveling quietly, lets out a wail.

Erwin thinks for a moment. "I'll stand up there against the wall and keep shouting his name as loud as I can. If he's in among those people, he should hear me in spite of all the noise."

I rack my brains. We thought we'd found Harald, but now everything's in doubt again. Erwin on the lookout with Rolfi in his arms? Impossible! In order to catch Harald he'd have to be lightning fast.

I take Rolfi back from him. I'll manage a visit to the toilet somehow, even with this little shrimp on my hands. Erwin dashes off.

"We'll be as quick as we can!" I call over my shoulder. The pack has to stay beneath the table.

With Rolfi in one arm and Lotte clinging to my other hand, I fight my way through to the ladies' room. Rolfi is squirming and whimpering. He's hungry and he wants his Mummy. And he's so heavy!

How much longer can this go on? I know one thing: I'm not leaving this air-raid shelter till the all-clear sounds.

The ladies' is a little brighter than the rest of the shelter, though there's only a bulb with a battered shade dangling from the ceiling. There's a crush in here, because the room is too small to hold so many people. Two women are sitting on their luggage in a corner, both wearing headscarves and one nursing her baby. No wonder they've settled down in here. It's scorching hot because of the central heating pipes, which run along the wall. I'm starting to sweat.

Agitation reigns here too. The news that it's possible to leave the shelter has spread fast. Should one go or not? It's still daylight outside, but soon it'll be dark. Why hasn't the all-clear sounded? Maybe the siren has broken down and nobody knows it yet?

Several women decide to leave. Quick, quick! Perhaps the exit will suddenly be barred again!

The doors of the two cubicles open and close, open and close. Women and girls are lined up in front of them. There's a third door in the corner with nobody in front of it. Great! We station ourselves outside.

A girl in the line-up beside us grins. "You'll have a long wait," she says.

I realize that we're standing in front of the door to a broom closet, probably full of cleaning things. How could I have been so stupid, especially when I'm in such a rush!

Luckily, a woman in line lets me go first, probably because I've got Rolfi and Lotte with me. I give her a grateful nod and push Lotte into the cubicle. She wants me to come in with her and clings to me.

I'm on the point of losing my temper with her—it's on the tip of my tongue to say: "You're getting on my nerves, Lotte!"—but I restrain myself. If she's had a nanny all her life, she's probably never had to do anything by herself. Maybe she's a spoiled brat, but it seems she's scared I'll go out and leave her while she's alone in the cubicle. With a sigh, I promise to remain standing outside.

"I'll stick the toe of my shoe under the door," I whisper to her. "That'll show you I'm still here."

"Both shoes!" she pleads.

Both is an impossibility, I'd fall over backward. Besides, I've got Rolfi in my arms. Even Lotte can see that, but she takes a good look at my shoes before she lets go of me, presumably memorizing what they look like.

As soon as she's inside the cubicle I stand in front of the door and shove my left foot under it as far as it'll go.

"Don't be long," I groan, gritting my teeth. "I'm in a hurry too!"

She promises to be quick, but I can hardly hear her faint voice because Rolfi is yowling in my ear and some other little kids are bawling nearby. Two women add to the din, one of them scolding her children, the other complaining about the war.

"If it weren't for this confounded war I'd still have my café! It's all gone—just a heap of rubble and ashes, when I spent half my life building up the business! I worked like a slave, and for what? For what? It's all down the drain! If I could at least feel we're going to win the war, but the way things are now, we'll get nothing for all our efforts. Nothing! It's all been in vain!"

Other refugee women proceed to reel off all the things they've had to leave behind. One of them is a landowner's wife mourning the loss of her estate. "A big house and five hundred acres of land!" she wails. "The finest stud farm you've ever seen—it's been in our family for six generations! And the horses, the horses! Thoroughbreds, every last one!"

"Hurry up, Lotte!" I call imploringly.

"There's no paper!" she calls back, sounding horrified.

That's all I need. I struggle to restrain my anger and impatience. Where on earth can I find some toilet paper?

A delighted exclamation from inside the cubicle: "I've just remembered! There's some in my coat pocket—Marta put it there!"

Thank heavens. I hear a rustling sound. Being a refugee, Lotte is bound to be wearing several layers of clothes like us. This is going to take a while.

I glance across at the sink near one corner. A single sink for all these women, not to mention their children! The faucet is left running all the time. A young woman splashes her face in feverish haste and applies some makeup, but the mirror is cracked—you can only see bits of yourself. There's a shaft leading upward in the opposite corner, presumably to ground level. A dim ray of daylight is slanting down through it, so there must be a window in the outer wall or some glass bricks set into the pavement. If Otto or Fritz were here—they're our school janitor's fourteen-year-old twins—they'd stand on tiptoe under the shaft and try to look up the skirts of the women walking past overhead. They tried to peek into the girls' changing room when we were getting dressed after gym, but they didn't dare do it again after we complained to their father.

A wash would be nice. I haven't had one since we left home. The snowflakes falling in the plaza are the only form of water to have touched my face. The train was so crowded, it was hard to get to the toilet, and anyway, the faucet over the little sink had run dry. All I did in the train was comb my hair. "What lovely long hair you have, Gisel," Mummy said when I undid my braids and combed them out...

Her labor pains hadn't started then. She combed the boys' hair while I was braiding mine again.

"Are you still there, Gisel?" Lotte asks anxiously from inside the cubicle.

"You can see the toe of my shoe," I tell her. "Besides, you can hear Rolfi crying."

"I don't know his voice well enough," she says plaintively.

The cubicle next door becomes vacant. There's no one waiting outside, so I seize the opportunity to dash inside. What a relief!

A piercing cry from Lotte's cubicle: "Gisel! Where are you?"

The noise outside dies away. The people standing around and sitting on their luggage are probably wondering what's wrong.

"Be quiet, Lotte!" I call. "I'm in here!"

I put Rolfi on the floor, pull down my tracksuit bottoms and all that's underneath them. Then I swivel sideways on the seat and stick my left foot under the partition. Lotte stops crying.

Phew! I can't help sighing at the thought of what I've saddled myself with. Lotte clings like a limpet. She might at least leave me in peace *now*!

8

ALL AT ONCE I HEAR ANOTHER VOICE—a very familiar voice—from outside the cubicles: "Gisel! Are you there?"

"Harald!" I call, on the verge of sobbing. "Wait, I'm coming!"

Lotte starts screaming because she can't see the tip of my shoe any longer, but I don't care, not now.

Harald's voice again, nearer this time: "Where are you, Gisel?"

"Here! Here in this cubicle!"

I tidy my clothing in a hurry, grab Rolfi and dash out. Harald is standing there among the women. He holds out his arms with a beaming smile. I pick him up, hug and kiss him. Lotte rushes out of her cubicle and clings to me.

"All right, you lot," I hear a woman say. "But now get out of the way. It's our turn."

And they thrust us aside.

"Where on Earth were you?" I ask. "I looked for you everywhere."

Harald points to the corner where the women in headscarves were sitting a few minutes ago. "Look, there's the bag."

He must have been sitting behind the women—or lying on the bag fast asleep.

"The food bag?" I'm bewildered. "How did it get here?"

"I never let it out of my sight," he says proudly.

I don't understand. Surely it was far too heavy for him to have lugged all the way from the station?

"A man stole it while I was standing on that pile of snow," Harald explains triumphantly. "I ran after him. He ran for the shelter with me right behind him. Then he went into the men's room. I guess he thought he'd lost me, but I followed him inside and told him to give it back. The other men believed me—they took the bag away from him and gave it to me because I could tell them what was inside. Then I brought it in here."

"But it was far too heavy for you!"

"I dragged it behind me, out of the men's room and into the ladies. I knew I'd be safe from him in here. I sat down in that corner, on top of the bag, to wait for the all-clear, but I fell asleep. Your voice woke me up."

"I must let Erwin know!" I shout.

But before I can open the door to the main shelter, a woman dashes in.

"There's another bunch coming!" she yells. She must mean enemy bombers. No time for questions. Should I go and take the children with me or stay put? The bag of food is in here, it would slow us down.

"Lotte," I say. "Run to Erwin as fast as you can and tell him to come right away. Tell him Harald is here!"

She starts to cry and shakes her head. I suppose she thinks it's a sneaky way of getting rid of her.

"Then stay here with Harald and Rolfi," I tell her angrily. "I'll go myself."

She clings to my coat.

"Let *me* go," says Harald, preparing to leave.

Lose him a second time? No, now that I've got him back I'm not letting him out of my sight!

I think feverishly. Should we all go together and give Erwin the news? But the food bag is still lying in the corner. We've got to keep that with us, no matter what!

I go over to the heavy bag and pick it up, making for the door.

Two women push ahead of us. One of them is carrying two children, a baby and a little boy of Rolfi's age. They're halfway out the door when someone bumps into them.

"Look where you're going, you idiot!" I hear them shout.

It's Erwin with the backpack. He's standing in the doorway looking agitated.

"The bombers are coming!" he gasps. "You can hear them already!"

He catches sight of Harald. His mouth falls open in surprise. "You're here?"

Harald beams at him and points to the bag of food. I don't know what to do or think of first. Rolfi stretches his arms out to Erwin. Lotte's nose is running again. Just then, the last remaining woman—no, a girl a little older than myself—emerges from one of the cubicles. She pushes past Erwin and hurries out.

"Where to now?" Erwin asks impatiently. "Out there or in here?"

I can hear a faint hum. It sounds almost like the distant thunder of guns we heard in the past few weeks. It was almost inaudible at first, except when the wind was blowing from the east, but later on, unless the weather was stormy, we could hear it all the time.

I glance through the open door. There aren't many people left in the main shelter—the benches around the walls are almost deserted—but the woman in the fox fur is still sitting on her canvas chair and people are streaming back inside.

"They're coming!" someone shouts.

I hear muffled explosions.

"Holy Mary, Mother of God, pray for us!" cries a woman sitting on the bench between the exit and the changing table. Her voice goes echoing around the walls.

"They must be a long way off," says someone. "Maybe in the industrial district on the other side of the river."

"People live there too," says the air-raid warden, quickly shutting the door to the outside again.

A piercing whistle. It grows louder, then ends with a big explosion. That means the bombs are getting closer. The door frame creaks and the cubicle doors rattle. I can scarcely breathe, Rolfi is clinging to me so tightly. Breaking out in a sweat, I pull Erwin into the ladies' and shut the door to the main cellar.

Then comes a whistling sound so shrill that it hurts my ears, followed by a thunderous crash that leaves me temporarily dazed. The whole building gives a lurch. I see Erwin tumble over backward and have trouble staying on my feet. Rolfi clings to me like a spider monkey; Lotte is screaming with her hands over her ears.

What's that rumbling? It sounds as if a violent thunderstorm has broken out above our heads. Girders creaking, concrete crumbling. Plaster trickles from the ceiling, chunks of mortar rain down, cracks appear in the walls. Harald lets out a yell as a fragment hits him on the head.

And then the light goes out, leaving us in utter darkness.

Outside in the main room it sounds as if a whole mountain of rubble is being unloaded. Screams ring out, metal creaks and groans. Something very, very heavy comes crashing down, probably onto the concrete floor, and the crash reverberates around the walls. The screams stop abruptly. Then, with a snapping, splintering sound, something collapses against the bathroom door.

9

I COWER DOWN, confronted by an infinity of darkness. I'm afraid of the dark—always have been—and would rather keep my eyes shut. My first thought: Are the children all right?

I can feel Rolfi. He's panting and clinging to my coat.

So the two of us are still alive.

Something nudges my foot. I put out my hand. It's Erwin's leg. He's there too. I'm about to speak to him when Lotte whimpers: "Gisel? Where are you?"

"Here," I say as calmly as I can. My mouth is full of dust. I swallow hard. "Don't be scared, everything's going to be all right."

That's what Mummy always says when something bad happens.

It's nonsense, of course. Unless I'm much mistaken, we're in a really tricky situation—buried alive—but there's no need for her to know that.

A hand touches my face. It can only be Lotte's.

"Hey, stop that," I say. "You poked me in the eye."

"Turn on the lights!" she demands.

"Turn them on yourself—if you can." There's a roaring in my

ears. My head is still in a whirl. What's the matter with Harald? I remember seeing a lump of mortar hit him on the...

"Harald?" I call anxiously. "Where are you?"

"Something hit me on the head," I hear him groan. "It hurts..."

"Wait, I'm coming."

But Lotte grabs my arm and won't let go. She doesn't want to be all on her own. But I have to look after the others too. I'm not her mother and I'm not Marta, either!

"Let go of me, Lotte!" I snap at her.

Erwin is stirring. I hear him spit. His mouth must be full of dust too.

"I'll see to Harald," he mumbles. His voice comes from the spot where I last saw him. I hear him shuffling along—crawling, not walking. He calls and Harald answers.

"Let's feel your head," Erwin says hoarsely, "so I can tell if it's still in one piece."

I breathe a sigh of relief. We're all here.

How different it is when you can't see, only hear and touch things. Straining my ears in the darkness, I hear a pathetic "Ow! Ouch!" followed by Erwin's brief, businesslike report: "He's got a bump, that's all." Then he adds: "A bump and a half, though!"

"Is it bleeding?"

Apparently not. Harald will get over it. He's survived plenty of bumps and bruises before now.

"Come over here, Harald," I say gently.

So we're all alive. No one is badly hurt. The worst that Harald can have is a concussion. Now we must make sure we *stay* alive.

I notice only now that my eyes are still shut. I open them, but

I might as well have kept them shut because everything is dark. Everything except the luminous dial and hands of my wristwatch. It's nine minutes past four.

We're hunkered down against the wall between the door and the sink, four of us huddled together and Rolfi on my lap. Our backs are up against the radiator, which is far from comfortable, it's so hot. Should we try to find a better place? Not yet. My head is still ringing from the explosion, and the others must be in the same state. I'm surprised I can hear anything.

Nobody speaks for a few minutes. We can hear each other breathing, that's all, but it's a reassuring sound. First we need to get over the immediate shock. My head is starting to clear, and I try to assess our situation. We'll have to come to terms with this darkness—to live with it for as long as necessary.

Then something occurs to me. Isn't there a window in the shaft across from us, on the other side of the sink? It ought to be letting in at least a faint ray of light. It can't be dark at this hour, even in winter.

"I need a pee," says Harald.

It's the shock. I need one too, though I've only just gone. And poor Rolfi? He's wearing rubber pants over his diaper, which must be completely soaked by now.

"We're not short of toilets," I tell Harald. "You've got two to choose from."

"But I can't see!"

"You'll have to feel your way there."

Harald isn't afraid of the dark, not him! I hear him shuffling along, hear the grit crunching under his shoes. A cubicle door creaks open. He's made it.

Someone else is also groping around. It must be Erwin. He's dragging something across the floor. The backpack? No, it must be the bag I left somewhere near the door. He's dragging it toward the far wall.

"Erwin? What are you planning to do?" I ask.

"I'm going to take a look next door."

Typical of Erwin to be so practical. Why didn't I think of that? If we manage to get out of here, and if the main exit isn't blocked, we'll be all right. Then we can hurry back to the station, find Granny and have some of that Red Cross soup. Granny must be sick with worry by now. She doesn't even know if we made it to an air-raid shelter.

But those are big "ifs."

Even if all goes well, I'm not sure I could eat, though. I've lost my appetite and there's a dull pain in my stomach.

"I want to go outside where it's light!" Lotte wails.

She really starts bawling now.

"I've found the handle," Erwin announces, rattling it.

"Wait for me!" Harald calls from his cubicle.

"Let Erwin go first and see what it's like out there," I tell Harald. "Then he can come back for the rest of us."

He pulls the chain. I hear the toilet flush.

"The door won't open," Erwin says, panting hard. "It must be jammed."

"Wait," I call. "We'll try together."

I attempt to release myself from Lotte's grip. She screams with fear. I explain that I need her help and ask her to look after Rolfi for a bit, so that I can help Erwin.

She doesn't answer for a moment. Then, timidly: "I'd rather not."

"In that case," I say sharply, "manage by yourself! I've no time for kids who aren't prepared to help when necessary!"

"But it's so dark," she wails.

"It's dark for all of us. Darkness isn't so bad, you just have to cope with it. You'll manage—you'd have to if you were blind. Will you look after Rolfi for me?"

"I never have to help at home," she says. "Marta does all the work."

"Marta isn't here," I tell her firmly. "If something needs doing, we'll have to do it ourselves. You aren't a baby anymore, you're seven, and that's old enough to help. Here, hold Rolfi for me till we get that door open."

I hear her edge closer. Her hand brushes mine.

She takes him from me. "But don't let him go crawling off," I warn. "He could cut himself on something. Hold him tight so he doesn't get away."

"What if he cries?"

"Let him cry. It won't kill him."

Sure enough, Rolfi starts crying.

I straighten up and get to my feet. Not knowing which way to go to find Erwin, I call, "Where are you?" Four voices answer almost simultaneously, Rolfi's included. Yes, even our baby brother can answer that question. When he started to talk we used to call "Where are you?" and taught him to answer "Here!"

I'm the only one who doesn't need to answer that question. The others will always know where I am. I've removed my wristwatch and threaded the strap through a buttonhole in my coat. The little luminous dial is glowing in the middle of my chest. Now everyone can see it as long as I'm facing them.

I grope my way over to Erwin and run my hands over the door. I can't recall if it opens inward or outward.

"Outward," says Erwin.

We brace ourselves against the door and push with all our might.

"A pity Daddy isn't here," Erwin says breathlessly. "Or Grandpa Häusler. They'd get it open in a hurry."

"Gille!" Rolfi calls. That's his name for me. He can't say "Gisela" yet.

"He's trying to get away," Lotte squeals. "He wants to come to you! What shall I do?"

"Just hang onto him," I tell her

I can't be bothered with them now, the door is more important. There must be some debris wedged against it. I remember hearing something hit the door after the explosion. Where's the keyhole? Somewhere below the handle. If there's no key in it and the lights are still on outside, I should be able to see through the keyhole.

Nothing, not a glimmer. The main fuse must have blown.

Unless the whole building is in ruins!

Harald emerges from the cubicle. I hear him trip over the food bag and drag it out of the way.

"Help me, Harald!" Lotte calls plaintively.

Erwin and I confer. If we both take a run at the door and throw our weight against it, we may open it a crack. We hold hands and take four steps back. Right, now we should be the same distance from the door. Let's hope we're facing in the right direction. We may run full tilt into the wall otherwise, and that would hurt.

Ready, steady, go! We crash into the door together. I crack my elbow on the door frame, but it's protected by three layers of sleeve.

The door doesn't budge.

"There must be something massive wedged up against it," Erwin says.

So we're trapped in this ladies' toilet. The window in the shaft is no use, either. It must be blocked by a mound of debris, or some light would filter in.

We're trapped. In total darkness.

It isn't cold, though, thanks to the central heating. I feel the radiator. It's only lukewarm now, but the room is still like an oven. I'm sweating, I notice, and not only with fear.

A sudden sound. Very faint, very distant. I give a start and listen intently: it's the all-clear. The siren is still working. That sound can penetrate the thickest walls. People rejoice to hear it, I know that from back home. It means the enemy bombers have gone and they can leave their air-raid shelters.

But not us.

What happened to the people in the main room when the building took a direct hit? It wasn't deserted, and we heard those screams! What about the lady in the fox fur? She may have managed to escape, or we'd have heard her calling or knocking. Or would we?

The siren dies away. A leaden silence follows.

But isn't that a fire engine I can hear very faintly?

We're huddled close together again. I could weep but I mustn't;

the others might start crying too. Lotte especially. I swallow hard several times to clear my throat.

"What an adventure," I say. "We'll have lots to tell everyone when this is over."

"They won't believe us," Harald says.

Erwin sighs. "We'll have to survive before we can tell anyone about it."

"Don't talk nonsense!" I say sharply. "It isn't as if we're in danger here!"

I make up my mind to have a word with him when the others aren't listening, maybe when they're asleep. He can't use words like "survive" or Harald and Lotte will fly into a panic. And that would only make matters worse.

I take Rolfi back from Lotte. "There," I say. "You did well, after all."

"You mean *me*?" she asks timidly.

I realize that anything we say to each other in the darkness must be accompanied by a name, or no one will know who is being spoken to.

"Yes, you, Lotte," I tell her. "You were a great help."

She gives a little sob. I suspect she's very proud that I'm pleased with her. What sort of a home life can she have had if no one ever expected her to help?

It's so hot. I take off Rolfi's hat and stuff it into my overcoat pocket, which is now bursting at the seams. Odd that the central heating still seems to be working. Have they stoked it up again? I'm about to take off my coat and advise the others to remove a few layers when I hear Harald sniffing.

"I smell smoke," he says. "Can you smell it too?"

We all sniff. It's true, there really is a smell of smoke.

"Something seems to be on fire outside," Erwin says. "If they dropped some incendiary bombs, the whole town could be in flames."

He knows what he's talking about, but not from the newspapers. They hardly ever publish photos of bomb damage in German cities. And the newsreels never refer to anything but our so-called successes.

But all of us in secondary school are shown pictures of various kinds of bombs and taught what to do during an air raid. One time a young teacher assembled us in the schoolyard and showed us how to put out fires. We only had her for English, and we all burst out laughing, she looked so funny dressed up in a steel helmet and a transparent visor.

That was over a year ago, when none of us dreamed we would ever get caught up in a genuine air raid. It all seemed so remote in those days. Big German cities like Berlin and Hamburg had been raided lots of times by then, but the enemy surely wouldn't bomb a small out-of-the-way town. What would have been the point? It wasn't a major rail junction and there weren't any munitions factories there.

Those lousy British and Americans!

But aren't we doing the same thing to them? Aren't we showering places in England with bombs that don't care whether they land on soldiers or women and children?

I haven't seen anything about us Germans feeling bad about that!

In English class we read a story about an English girl. In English, of course. Her name was Susan, and I really took to her. We learned what goes on in English girls' schools and English families, and how English brothers and sisters and their friends get on together, and what the English do on Sundays, and what they like to eat and do, and so on. They aren't so very different from us.

Once I saw some English prisoners of war in our town. They didn't look like enemies. I always used to picture enemies as monsters so evil you couldn't mistake them for anything else, but if you'd dressed those Englishmen in German uniforms you'd never have known they were English! So why are we fighting them? That's what I kept wondering when we read that story about Susan.

"Will this place catch fire too?" Lotte asks anxiously.

"Rubble doesn't burn," I tell her. "Besides, fire travels upward, not downward, and we're in the cellar."

Reassure them, distract them, keep them occupied—that's Mummy's recipe in difficult situations. She did that with us in the train, even when her pains came. I seem to be succeeding.

But then Erwin makes another alarming contribution: "The potatoes in a campfire are right at the bottom, down among the ashes, but they get baked just the same."

"It couldn't possibly get that hot all the way down here," I say quickly. But he's frightened me. Are we like potatoes in the ashes? I wonder. Is it gradually getting hotter in here?

I don't think so. On the contrary, I suddenly feel cold. I'm shivering, in fact, but not because of the temperature. I'm shivering with fear. I mustn't draw attention to the warmth, or they might think the building is on fire.

"Now we'll have something to eat," I hear myself say to change the subject.

Somebody sighs with relief. Harald, from the sound of it. It's probably him that's dragging the bag over.

"If I hadn't kept following that thief," he says, "we wouldn't have anything to eat at all."

Of course: Erwin still hasn't heard about his heroic deed, and Harald is eager for a pat on the back from his big brother. To me, though, our search for Harald seems an eternity ago. His story is so unimportant now! How are we to get out of here? That's what I keep wondering.

We hunker down around the food bag. It doesn't matter where we sit, it's dark and dusty everywhere. Just as long as we don't sit on something sharp.

I grope in the bag, feel the apples, find the bag of sausages and hard-boiled eggs. A rustle of greaseproof paper: that must be the sandwiches. One of sausage and one of cheese apiece. I know that because I helped to butter and pack them. I keep one for myself and hand one to each of the others without checking what's in it. They're soon busy swapping. "Would you rather have cheese? Then give me one with sausage..."

It's lucky we can find our own mouths in the dark. There's nothing to be heard before long but contented munching noises. I share my cheese sandwich with Rolfi, breaking off bits of bread for him to feed himself.

"Eat slowly and chew it well," I tell everyone. "This is all you're getting for the moment. We don't know how long they'll take to dig us out of here. We'll have to make the food last."

"Isn't there anything to drink?" Lotte enquires in her squeaky voice.

Yes, the bag contains two half-empty bottles, one of elderberry juice, the other of milk. But the little we have must be strictly rationed. We don't know how long we'll have to manage on what we've got, so we'll have to watch every drop. Should we count the number of swallows? Then Erwin would get far more than Harald, and who knows if the children would stop after one mouthful? It's dark, after all, so someone might cheat.

That's no good. Each of us must get the same amount in a container of some kind.

But that presents the next problem: pouring in the dark. Will I spill some if I can't see? I rummage in the bag and bring out Rolfi's little enamel mug. I pour him some milk. He drinks it greedily, slurping away with gusto.

One bottle half full and one with even less than that—between five people. What if we have to stay down here for days? A shiver runs down my spine. What if we slowly die of thirst? It's an awful way to go, they say. One of the worst.

Then it occurs to me: we've got plenty of water! After all, I washed my hands in the sink just before the explosion, and I saw a lot of women cup their hands under the faucet and drink from them.

"Water!" I exclaim. " You can drink as much water as you like, there's plenty here. All you need do is find your way to the sink."

"Where is it?" Lotte asks in a timid voice.

"Along the wall on the other side from where we came in."

Harald has already set off.

"Found it, found it!" he calls proudly.

"Keep saying 'Aaaa' until I get to you," Erwin tells him. "Then you can have a drink and I'll guide the others."

Harald turns his "Aaaa" into an imitation of an air-raid siren.

"Stop it!" I tell him angrily. "I can't bear that sound!"

He falls silent. Erwin starts imitating the noise Granny makes when she's feeding the chickens: "Put-put-put-put-put...!"

I get up, bend over Rolfi, take him by both hands and steer him in the direction of the sound. Instead of clinging to my coat, Lotte rests her hand quite lightly on my arm. Does she trust me now? Even if she doesn't, she knows we're shut up in here. I couldn't give her the slip even if I wanted to.

She seems to have grown used to the darkness. I'd never have believed it.

10

ALL AT ONCE HARALD CALLS: "There isn't any water coming out!"

"Nonsense," I say. "It was still running when you flushed the toilet just now. If it's filling the tank, it must be coming out of the faucet. You can't have turned it on far enough."

The faucet squeaks. Erwin's "Put-put-put" dies away.

"Let me try," I hear him say.

The faucet squeaks again.

"There really isn't any water, Gisel," Erwin says. "I've turned it on as far as it'll go."

Unwilling to believe this, I get to the sink and try the faucet myself. Not even a drop.

"But it was gushing out before!" I say in dismay.

Erwin sighs. "It must be the bomb. It's broken the electrical wires after all."

"Then we'll manage without water," says Harald.

"Are you crazy?" Erwin exclaims. "Human beings need water; otherwise they die of thirst."

Silence. I can picture Harald's face.

"Are we going to die of thirst?" he asks.

Lotte grabs my arm. "I don't want to die!" she says tearfully.

I take a deep breath. What would Mummy say? She'd probably try to reassure the little ones so they're not frightened, but Mummy isn't here. I'm taking her place.

"I don't want to die either, Lotte," I tell her. "But you don't die of thirst as quickly as that. It takes a long time, and we'll be out of here well before then."

"But your tongue dries up," Erwin objects. "Our teacher told us that. Your whole throat dries up. You can't speak or swallow any more."

"Yes," I say lightly. "It's not very nice, but you get used to it. Anyway, it won't come to that. They'll dig us out tonight for sure— tomorrow morning at the latest."

"If your words were a bridge, I wouldn't cross it..." That's what Granny would say. I dearly wish Granny were here, helping us to be brave in the dark.

We return to our place by the radiator. I put everything back in the bag and zip it up again. We can't have a drink, not now. The contents of the two bottles combined can't add up to more than about four mugs.

"But does anyone know we're down here?" Lotte asks.

I stare in shock toward the sound of her voice. That hadn't occurred to me. No one may realize we're here. If so, they won't make any attempt to dig us out!

I need time to think.

Lotte's question seems to have sparked Harald's imagination. "Perhaps they'll listen for sounds," he says.

Then I remember the broom closet. It's bolted but not locked.

Erwin and I open it and root around inside. I find a scrubbing brush and Erwin grabs a broom. We use them to bang on the wall between the sink and the shaft. My shoe grates on something.

"It's not loud enough," Erwin says. "We need to shout from underneath the window. The glass has gone."

"How do you know?" I ask, puzzled.

"There's broken glass there."

Erwin can be really smart sometimes. I'd thought it was bits of the mirror, but that's still there.

"Right," I say. "Let's shout. Get beneath the window, all of you."

With Rolfi in one arm, I cautiously feel my way along the wall to the shaft. Soon I should feel glass underfoot.

There it is. "I've come to the broken glass!" I call to the others. "Don't go any farther!"

Why am I shouting? In a room this size they would all get the message even if I whispered.

"What shall we shout?" Erwin asks. "'Here we are!' or 'Hello!' or 'Come and get us!'?"

"'Help!' would be best," I tell him.

"You count up to three, then we'll shout," Erwin suggests. "All of us together, as loud as we can."

We pick up a rhythm: "Heeellp! Heeellp! Heeellp...!"

Everyone is bellowing like mad, Lotte included. She must be red in the face by now. Rolfi is the only one who's not shouting "Help!". He's just yelling, but it adds to the racket. I pat his hand while I shout.

The noise down here is deafening, but will they hear it up

there? They're bound to, if only a few buildings have been hit, but if the whole town was bombed the rescue teams and firefighters will have lots of buried shelters to check on. Ours will be only one of many. If so, our chances will be slim.

"I can't any more," gasps Erwin.

All this shouting has made me feel dizzy.

"That's enough!" I call.

Silence falls once more—the terrible silence that so clearly shows how isolated we are.

Suddenly, I hear a knocking sound. We all freeze, listening intently. Is someone outside the door? Is someone signaling on the floor above us?

"It's coming from over there," Harald says, as if we can see where he's pointing in the dark.

I've located it now too. It's coming from the broom closet wall.

"That's the men's room in there," Erwin says.

Is someone trapped in the men's room? That would mean we aren't on our own down here!

"Quick," Erwin says. "We need to answer."

It hasn't taken us long to get used to shuffling across the tiled floor, feeling for obstacles with our feet: walls, cubicle doors, the broom closet, chunks of mortar.

We haven't been over here since the bomb landed. There wasn't any reason to come here.

We pound on the tiled wall with our fists. It makes almost no sound. The younger ones' efforts are even less effective, but at least it keeps them busy.

Then Harald has an idea. He takes off his shoe and hammers

on the tiles with the heel. That's louder. The others follow suit, all except for Rolfi, who's clinging to my leg.

Erwin gets a dustpan out of the broom closet. He's so eager to get to work, he elbows me hard in the chest. The edge of the dustpan catches me under the chin.

"Careful!" I say indignantly.

My chin is bleeding, I suspect, but not badly. I wipe it on the back of my hand while Erwin starts banging the dustpan against the wall. I join in with my shoe. Can we be heard on the other side?

We stop to listen. Will the person or persons reply?

Rolfi, scared by all the noise, has started to cry. I shush him.

We hear a distinct sound: someone is knocking. But words? Shouts? No. The wall must be very thick.

At least we know there's someone in the men's room. Whether one person or several, they're still alive. We know they can't get out like us, but that's all.

No, that isn't all. We also know they must be in the dark without water, and that they probably won't have any blankets or food. After all, how many people take such things to the toilet with them?

I notice that the room hasn't become any warmer. It still smells of burning, but a smell like that tends to linger, as I know only too well. The kitchen stank for ages when I burned some fried potatoes! The good news is that we don't appear to be in danger from fire any longer.

As bad as things seemed a short while ago, they could be a whole lot worse.

We're still alive and kicking!

I feel wildly exhilarated all of a sudden. I clap my hands and call out, "Let's dance, children! Dance and sing: 'We're still alive, still alive, still alive!'"

My enthusiasm infects Lotte and Harald. I can tell from the sound of their feet that they're turning on the spot as they chant the words. Even Rolfi joins in, shouting.

Lotte amazes me. She seems to have completely adjusted to her situation in such a short time. How quick she has been to learn so many new things!

Erwin gropes his way along the wall and bumps into me.

"Why don't you join in?" I whisper.

"I don't feel like singing," he replies.

"Then do it for the little kids. We've got to keep their spirits up. And you have to be more careful about saying things that will frighten them! Surely you wouldn't prefer them to cry for Mummy all the time?"

He joins in, but he chants, "Where's the crack?" instead of "We're still alive!" It isn't long before we're all chanting, "Where's the crack? Where's the crack?" with all our might. Then Rolfi starts crying again. He must be overtired, and the darkness probably confuses him.

"What made you sing 'Where's the crack?'" I ask Erwin.

He says he's had an idea. When the bomb landed, just before the lights went out, he noticed some cracks opening in the wall. If one of them is big enough, it may help us to talk with whoever is trapped in the men's room.

It's worth a try. Erwin and I run our fingers over the upper wall while the two younger ones check the lower part. Erwin even fishes a bucket out of the broom closet. He turns this upside down and stands on it, then reaches as high as he can. We discover some cracks, but they're too small.

Then Lotte calls out: "I've found something!"

She really has found something, but not a crack. Projecting a little way from the wall, right in the corner and roughly at knee height, is a metal pipe. It has a plug on the end—a screw cap.

Does it run right through the wall to the other side?

The cap is hard to unscrew—it obviously hasn't been removed for a long time. Erwin and I take turns. He gets it off at last, but it slips through his fingers, goes rolling across the floor, and winds up someplace among the debris. We both crouch down and bump heads. I nudge Erwin aside and peer into the pipe.

"Nothing to be seen," I gasp. "It must be blocked."

"What idiots we are!" Erwin exclaims. I hear him smack his head. "It must be dark at the other end too!"

He pushes me out of the way.

"Hello, hello!" I hear him call. "Anyone there?"

"Now put your ear to the pipe!" I whisper.

"I'm doing that," he whispers back. "I can't hear anything, though."

"Maybe there's a cap on the other end too."

"Shall I have a try?" asks Harald. "I can shout a lot louder than you."

"Shut up!" Erwin growls.

So the pipe is no use. We can only communicate by knocking.

All at once I hear Erwin say excitedly, "Yes?" Then: "Erwin Beck."

We listen.

I can only hear what Erwin says. He's answering someone's questions. "I'm twelve."—"Five of us."—"No, our mother isn't here."—"Yes, just us children."—"Fifteen, twelve, six and eighteen months. And a girl who isn't our sister. I don't know how old she is."—"No, not that either."—"No, nor that."

A long silence.

"Is he still speaking?" Harald asks.

Erwin doesn't answer. Then, suddenly: "Yes, we have."—"Yes, we will. Speak to you later."

"Well," he says, and I hear him getting to his feet. "Now we know." He sighs. "I'm really stiff."

"What is it?" I say eagerly.

"Things are even worse next door than they are here. Half the ceiling has collapsed onto the urinals. No lights or water in there either. It was a direct hit, he says, and the air-raid shelter has been buried. He doubts there's anyone alive out there."

I can't help thinking of the woman in the hat and the fox fur. And the air-raid warden who shut the door at the last minute.

"What about other people in the men's room?" I ask tensely.

There aren't any.

"He's a soldier," Erwin continues. "He can only move with difficulty because his left leg is smashed. Part of the ceiling fell on it. He managed to scrape away a lot of rubble and get his leg free, but it's badly broken. He has to drag it behind him, which hurts—that's why he took a while to get to the pipe. It bled a lot to begin with, but the bleeding has stopped. He had no idea anyone was in here—didn't hear us until we all shouted for help. He used one of his boots to bang on the wall. His name is Rockel. He says he'll be in touch again at seven o'clock tonight."

"Poor Herr Rockel," Lotte sighs.

I'm thinking the same thing. He must be in a very bad way with a shattered leg. And no doctor to help. I feel quite sick when I think how much it must hurt. And he's all alone in there!

"Did he say anything about rescue?" I ask. "When does he think they'll get us out?"

"He says he's sure they'll find us, by tomorrow morning at the latest. We need to make sure we're heard, that's all. When a public air-raid shelter gets hit, he says, the rescue teams search for survivors there first."

That's reassuring news. Herr Rockel ought to know, being a soldier. I sit down with my back against the wall and my knees pulled up.

"Hello, hello!" we hear Harald call down the pipe. "My name's Harald. I go to school already!"

I bend over, intending to pull him away. Herr Rockel needs peace and quiet in his condition. He seems to be answering, though, because Harald's brief silences are punctuated by "Yes," "No," "Does it hurt a lot?" and "Something hit me on the head, now I've got a bump there."

When he offers to tell Rockel some jokes, however, I really do haul him away from the pipe.

Harald is indignant. "I only wanted to take his mind off things!"

Rolfi squeezes himself between my knees, whimpering. His little bottom is probably sore. I should have changed his diaper ages ago, but I'm so exhausted. I'll doze off if I'm not careful.

Someone crouches down beside me. It's Lotte.

"I feel so sorry for him," she says, "lying there on the cold floor with no blanket and nothing to eat or drink..."

"He's been on my lap most of the time," I tell her, thinking she means Rolfi. "Besides, he's had a whole mug of milk..."

But she means Herr Rockel.

I feel sorry for him too, but I don't think there's anything we can do.

I can't stifle a loud yawn.

"Herr Rockel is badly hurt," Lotte says reproachfully, "and all you can do is yawn!"

It's easy for you to talk, I think. You don't have any responsibilities. You've only yourself to worry about.

I give another yawn. Oh yes, Rolfi. It's time I...time I...

Rolfi, Harald, Erwin and I are sitting in the train with our luggage. All our favorite possessions are there, including my ice skates and my doll Heidi. Erwin's football, too, and Harald's teddy. And our clothes and shoes, and Mummy's precious china, and the French clock, and all our books—our books, how wonderful!—and all our furniture, carpets and curtains, and all our pictures— even the garden tools and the laundry basket and the rabbit hutch and the hen coop, and the whole house itself, complete with garden. And Bella is standing in the middle of the compartment, whimpering with joy and wagging her tail!

But Mummy and Granny are missing. We thread our way through the luggage to the window. Our train is just pulling out of a station. We catch sight of Mummy and Granny on the platform. They want to come too, but the door won't open. They run along beside the train, but it's gathering speed. We shout, and they shout back. Nobody helps us because there's nobody here in the compartment but us children. Mummy and Granny fall farther and farther behind, and looming up beyond them is a dark wall of cloud engulfing our village. I scream, and scream, and scream...

11

SOMEBODY GRIPS MY SHOULDER. "Gisel?"

I wake up with a start and open my eyes. Nothing, just darkness. "Erwin?"

"Are you tired too?" he asks. I feel him squat down beside me.

I pinch my leg hard. We can't afford to be tired at the same time, the little ones would be left by themselves.

"No," I tell him, trying to sound wide awake. "I was tired before, but I'm not any more."

"Well, I am," he says with a sigh. He asks the time and I tell him: ten past six.

"I'm going to lie down in the corner beside that pipe," he says. "Wake me at seven."

I promise.

"Put a blanket under you," I call after him.

I hear him rummaging in the backpack. He calls to Lotte and Harald. "Here, take your blankets for the night!"

It's lucky he didn't leave the pack under the changing table. At least we've got blankets. We'd freeze in here without them, because the fire must have burned out. It'll get even colder now.

A blanket is passed to me from hand to hand.

Granny doesn't have a blanket because the backpack is here. Still, she isn't shut up in a toilet below ground. She should be able to go somewhere and get warm, assuming she wasn't hurt. I can't bear to even think about that possibility.

She's probably worried sick about us. I wonder if she's managed to get in touch with Grandpa and Grandma Glottke. But maybe she didn't want to frighten them by telling them she doesn't know where we are.

Harald trips over me, but I catch him in time. That makes us laugh. I laugh louder than usual, to cheer everyone up.

I grope around in the backpack and fish out a clean diaper, a knitted sleeper, a little sweater and some thick socks. There, that's Rolfi taken care of. I decide to hold him over the toilet every couple of hours. If I do that, the four diapers should last him for as long as we're stuck down here. At least, I hope so!

I feel in the pack's four little side pockets and find a comb, a bag containing our toothbrushes and toothpaste, and ointment for Rolfi's bottom. I might have known it: Granny always packs things where they're easy to get at.

In the main compartment is something I'd thought was in the suitcases: our two photo albums. So we haven't lost them after all! I've always loved looking at them. It's fascinating to see what you looked like as a baby or when you started school. Or what Daddy and Mummy looked like as children. Or Grandpa and Granny on their wedding day. If it weren't for these albums, I wouldn't know what my great-grandparents looked like, or what kind of clothes they wore when they dressed up for a party or a visit to the photographer's studio. But what's the use of photos when it's pitch-black?

When I push the bag aside, rather roughly, something goes clunk. It sounds metallic. What can it be? A can? A spoon? I'm too tired to check.

With Rolfi under one arm, I grope my way into a cubicle and undress him. He's soaking wet, of course. There's the usual smell too. It seems stronger here than at home, as if your nose becomes more sensitive when you can't see a thing.

I perch Rolfi on the seat and hold him there in the hope that he realizes where he is in spite of the darkness and knows what's expected. I don't have to wait long, fortunately. Next, I spread out my blanket on the floor and lay Rolfi down on it. He protests, but it doesn't do him any good.

It's not easy to smear ointment on a baby's bottom in the dark, and his hands keep getting in the way. Some of the stuff gets on my face and I have to wipe it off, but eventually I get him freshly bundled up again.

It's so cramped in this cubicle! I keep bumping into the partition walls. Why didn't I leave the door open? No one can see us.

Have I forgotten to flush? I sniff to check. Confound this darkness! Out of habit, I feel for the dangling chain and give the handle a pull. No use, there's no water left. Harald flushed the toilet earlier, of course.

Taking Rolfi by the hand, I find my way over to Harald and Lotte, who are sitting with their backs against the wall next to the radiator and playing a game of some kind—an amusing game, from the sound of it. I can't see what they're doing, just hear them laughing, so I ask them to explain it to me. Apparently, they each hold out their left hand and pull it back quickly when they think their opponent is about to strike, simultaneously trying to smack the other person's outstretched hand with their right hand. According to Harald, the score stands at eleven to nine in his favor.

I'm glad they're so relaxed. They probably don't realize what a mess we're in.

I'm cold, and no wonder, the radiator has cooled off completely. We'll need our blankets. I wrap half of mine around me, saving the other half for Rolfi when he gets tired. "What about you two?" I ask Harald and Lotte. "Don't you want to wrap yourselves up in your blankets?" No, they haven't reached that stage yet—they're still too engrossed in their game in the dark.

Rolfi tugs at my arm. He wants to play too, but with me. He has no idea how tired I am.

I suddenly remember the broken glass on the floor. It could be dangerous if the children trip and fall. I need to sweep it up, but I'll have to hand over Rolfi first. I keep him occupied until Lotte and Harald get tired of their game and I can give him to them.

"Take good care of him!"

Wrapping my blanket around me, I set off to get the broom. I remember Erwin putting it back in the broom closet after we banged on the wall. I fumble for the bolt but can't find it. Completely exhausted, I sink to the floor.

By now it must be dark outside. I wonder how Mummy is, and the baby. Maybe they'll get to Dresden before us. And Granny? I wonder where she is, and if she's all right. I wish we could let her know we're all alive, so she doesn't worry.

My last waking thought: the closet door isn't as cold as the tiled wall.

I'm standing on Flagstaff Hill, on parade with my fellow members of the German Girls' League. The Hitler Youth detachment from our village is also there, drawn up in a square. If it was light, we could see the village down below us. Fluttering overhead is the red and white flag with the black swastika in the center.

The summer solstice festival is a solemn, impressive occasion. A big, crackling bonfire sends tongues of flame leaping high into the air in front of us. Someone in a mustard-yellow uniform is delivering a speech in which the words "our Führer," "fighting spirit," "the Greater German Reich" and "final victory" are repeated over and over. We all join in a rousing chorus.

I can see other bonfires blazing on the hills nearby. I'm overcome by a wonderful feeling of togetherness. How I regret not being a boy! I'd like to fight for my country and help to win the war. How proud I am to be German! How strong I feel!

My heart overflows with joy as the flames leap ever higher. Uncontrollable now, they set fire to our village and the other villages around—even to the town on the horizon. There are flames wherever I look! The fire belongs to no one any more, not to us or the speaker on Flagstaff Hill. What now? For God's sake, what will happen now?

All at once it becomes cold, terribly cold. I can see Granny standing in the rhubarb bed and digging away like mad. Now, in the middle of winter! The rhubarb bed gets turned every year, but not until the end of March, when the ground has thawed out. Despite this, she's wielding the hoe in a frenzy and glancing repeatedly at her wristwatch. Sprouting from the soil in springtime are huge green leaves with thick, juicy stems that we chew when we're thirsty. Mummy stews them. But nothing is growing there now. The rhubarb bed is bare, the earth as hard as concrete.

Beyond it lies the Häuslers' farmhouse, and beyond that the pine forest. That's where the sun rises, so it always gets light there first, but the sky above the forest is dark. The sight of a gathering storm has always frightened me. You know it's going to be bad, but you don't know how bad!

Granny's solitary figure is outlined against the dark, menacing bank of cloud. I can make out something on the ground beside her—something wrapped up in the old sheet of oilcloth from the garden table. It must be the French clock.

The shaft of Granny's hoe snaps. She picks up a spade and tries to drive it into the ground, but it's no use. Grandpa Häusler suddenly appears with a pickax. Clods of frozen soil go flying into the air like a fountain, but then he gives up too.

Now, like something from a speeded-up film, Granny and Grandpa Häusler scuttle into our house and down to the potato cellar, where they dig up the mud floor. He digs a deep hole and helps her to bury the oblong oilcloth package. She rakes and sweeps the loose mud back into the hole. Then they both stamp it down until no one would know there had been a hole there at all.

A lot of chunks of mud are left over. As if they're potatoes, Granny carries them up to the kitchen and puts them on to boil. We sit down around the table, and sure enough, the chunks have turned into potatoes! Yellow, fragrant boiled potatoes. We wolf them down, skins and all.

At some point I glance at Daddy's desk and see the French clock standing where it always did. It's ticking—a familiar, well-remembered sound.

So what is it that lies buried downstairs, Granny? What's inside that oblong oilcloth package?

I feel scared. I don't know why, but my heart is pounding.

Now I see our living room. Strange men in foreign uniforms are sitting around our living room table, talking in a foreign language. They raise jars of our preserves to their mouths and slurp the contents, munching and smacking their lips. Standing guard beside the door is a man wearing a fur hat and holding a big knife between his teeth. He grins at me. He looks just like the diabolically grinning Russian on the posters displayed all over our village and the local town. I don't remember what it said underneath them, but they were designed to show what subhuman creatures the Russians are.

Mummy's best china is lying on the carpet beside the table, smashed to smithereens. The glass over Mummy and Daddy's wedding picture has also been smashed. The windowpanes are shattered and the curtains are hanging in shreds. So, in some places, is the wallpaper. Most of the books have been tipped off the shelves and are scattered across the floor, and the French clock is missing from the desk. That's safe, though. It's buried deep in the cellar.

Bella is howling pathetically outside. The Russian on guard draws his pistol and takes aim through the window. A shot rings out. Bella's howls cease abruptly.

Where's Mummy? And Granny? I bend down and peer beneath the table. Someone is lying there. I catch sight of two feet, see the soles of two slippers. They're Granny's! Oh, Granny!

Paralyzed with fear, I gasp for breath. Mummy! Where are you?
"Mummeeee!"

12

"GISEL?"

I wake with a start and fling the blanket aside. Who called me? Erwin. He's bending over me and I can feel his warm breath on my forehead.

"Take a look at your watch and see what time it is," he says.

Ten past eight.

"Good heavens," I exclaim, "I've slept for an hour and a half!"

"An hour and a half?" I can tell from his voice that he's grinning. "Fourteen hours, more like. It's ten past eight in the morning."

"Nonsense!" I say, getting to my feet.

I'm completely dazed. Have I really slept the night away? I've never done such a thing before.

On the other hand, I've never had a day like yesterday before.

"Ssh, the others are still asleep. I got woken up last night by Rockel yelling down the pipe at half past seven. He was afraid we were all dead—a gas leak or something. Then I realized I hadn't heard anything from you. I was so scared, I told him I couldn't talk then, but I'd call him later."

"And then?"

"I made my way along the wall toward the radiator, because I remembered you were there earlier. I nearly tripped over Harald. The three of them were asleep on the same blanket: Harald and Lotte with Rolfi between them, all snuggled up together. They'd spread another blanket over themselves. Did you put them to bed like that?"

"No." I shake my head in surprise.

"I bent over them and listened. They were fast asleep."

I'm dumbfounded. Did they really do that by themselves? Lotte amazes me. When I think how timid she was yesterday afternoon...

"Then I searched the rest of the room for you," Erwin goes on. "I found you here, against the broom closet. Not dead, but sound asleep. After that I went to the toilet. It stinks a bit, but I can't help that." He pauses. "I tried to stay awake—Rolfi might have needed something, after all—but I dozed off anyway. I couldn't sleep properly, though. I kept waking up and listening to make sure you were still alive—Rockel scared me with his gas leak idea—but everything was fine. The blanket slipped off Harald once because Lotte had pulled it over her side and Rolfi was lying on the bare tiles. I fixed that, then I thought I should call Herr Rockel. But when I looked at your watch it was half-past three in the morning. So I let him sleep." Another pause. "Lucky your watch glows in the dark, or we wouldn't have a clue what time it is..."

I try to imagine what it would be like, a timeless world where no one knows if it's day or night. It would be almost like being dead!

"You woke me up a couple of times," I hear Erwin say. "You shouted in your sleep. For Mummy. You were groaning too."

It's coming back to me: the dark wall of cloud, the feeling of dread. Those were horrible nightmares!

"Rockel woke me at eight," Erwin goes on quietly. "He's got a voice like a foghorn."

"Well?" I ask. "How is he today?"

"He's cold and thirsty, and his leg hurts. Today, he says, they'll be checking any public air-raid shelter that was hit. Oh yes, and he'd like to talk with you at nine o'clock."

With me? I wonder why, but I'll find out soon. I'm really impressed by Erwin. To think that he took on the responsibility for the little ones during the night—that he didn't wake me and leave it to his older sister!

"Erwin," I tell him, "you deserve a medal for being so reliable. Now get some sleep. I've had plenty."

He nods and yawns. "I'll bed down in the corner, near the pipe. Wake me up if anything happens."

I FEEL SO ASHAMED. Erwin is only twelve and I left him in charge, all on his own, by simply falling asleep. Today I'll let him rest and take twice as much care of the others.

I try to sort out my thoughts. What day is it today? We left home on Friday. The first night we spent in the train, the second night down here in the cellar, so it must be Sunday. Ah, Sundays, glorious Sundays! We're always allowed to stay in bed till nine—as long as we aren't on duty and the German Girls' League doesn't have to parade in the square outside the church. I didn't like being on duty on a Sunday. Sundays are a kind of family day, a private day.

On weekdays, we three school kids have to get up at six, and not just to wash, comb our hair, clean our teeth and have breakfast. We all have chores to do. Erwin has to bring wood from the barn for the tiled stove in the living room and coal from the cellar for the kitchen range. He also has to feed Bella and the chickens and rabbits. Harald has to clean all the shoes and I'm responsible for washing and dressing Rolfi, then feeding him, which takes quite a while. Then we have breakfast and go to school.

But on Sundays everything is different. Mummy looks after Rolfi and the animals, so we can sleep in. I don't wake up much later than on weekdays, actually, but on Sundays I read. That's my favorite thing to do. I always keep a book under my pillow and I'm a very fast reader. I haven't had much time lately, because I've had to help Mummy a lot with Daddy away, especially since she's been expecting another baby.

I'm usually so tired at night, I can only read a page or two before my eyelids droop. But I always have time on Sunday mornings— unless I'm on duty—and then I gorge myself on books. Especially in wintertime.

I can't read down here. There aren't any books, and anyway, it's pitch-black.

All I can do while the others are asleep is think.

What should I think of? Granny? Mummy and the baby? Our situation? I keep thinking about that anyway, whether I want to or not. I'd rather think of something nice.

Like my birthday. If today is Sunday, it must be tomorrow. Then I'll be sixteen. If we'd stayed at home, I'd have had a cake with sixteen candles. What would I have been given? A book, for sure—maybe even two. Books are Granny's responsibility. You can still buy books. I've asked for *The Volga Children*. Granny said she'd try to get it for me.

Elsi raved about *The Volga Children*, which she borrowed from someone. It's about five children from the Volga district whose parents are arrested and imprisoned by the new rulers of Russia after the First World War, and who decide to escape to Germany. The journey takes weeks, and it's extremely dangerous, but they get there at last and are reunited with their parents, who have also escaped and fled to Germany.

And Mummy? She's bound to have knitted me something. A sweater, maybe? She usually knits at night, after we've gone to bed. She's unraveled Granny's old dark green cardigan and moistened and stretched the wool to straighten it—I know that much. If she's knitted it into a sweater, that means the sweater will be green. With colored stripes, of course, because she could only unravel the best parts of Granny's cardigan. The elbows were worn through and the front was all matted. Mummy still has lots of of colored wool leftovers in her sewing drawer, so she's bound to have used some of those. Maybe the Häuslers gave her something to unravel too.

So...a new sweater? I'll have to wait and see. I don't even know if she brought it with her. Sweaters are warm, though—just the thing for a refugee like me, especially in winter. The chances of it being in our luggage are pretty good.

In our luggage? That's a laugh! We had to leave our suitcases behind in the station. They won't be there any more. Still, it's nice to dream of a new sweater.

Will the Häuslers have remembered to give Mummy a birthday present for me in all that confusion? I doubt it. For the past few years they've given me a fancy cup and saucer for my bottom drawer. They belonged to Great-Grandma Häusler. I'm not too keen on fancy cups. You can only drink out of them, after all, but Mummy says they're fine porcelain—something nice to save for later.

But all the cups have been left at home. Plus the one I should have been given tomorrow. Refugees can't afford to take useless ballast with them.

The same with *The Volga Children*, probably. I'm sorry about that— very sorry! Still, Grandpa and Grandma Glottke may have bought me a book—they know how much I love reading. And there's the sewing box Grandpa has made me!

I straighten up with a groan. I'm aching all over, probably because I fell asleep sitting up. The air smells nasty and it's very chilly. It was warmer in here last night. Of course, the radiators are as cold as ice—everything's broken. Today I'll get the children to hop on the spot to warm up.

I grope my way into the cubicle nearest the broom closet. There's less debris on this side of the room. It smells really awful in here, but there's nothing to be done, it'll smell even worse in a minute! That reminds me of the soldier next door. It sounded as if all of the stalls there were buried in rubble.

As I lower the seat, it slips through my fingers and comes crashing down on the toilet bowl. That will wake up the little ones!

Sure enough, it did. I'm just tiptoeing out of the cubicle when Rolfi calls out. "Gille!"

"Why is it still so dark?" Lotte asks sleepily.

"Cellars are always dark," I tell her.

"In *our* cellar you can turn on the light," she retorts.

"You don't feel the cold as much in the dark," I say reassuringly. "It's better like this."

That's nonsense, but perhaps she'll swallow it. I know one thing: it's going to take a lot of ingenuity to pass the time and keep them happy.

For how long? Maybe till tomorrow. Or the day after tomorrow. Or the day after that...Maybe till we...

"Snuggle up for a bit longer, all of you," I say, sounding studiously cheerful. "Today you can sleep as long as you like. It's Sunday."

They don't mention being thirsty, thank goodness. I'm trying not to think about those two half-empty bottles, but I'm getting more and more thirsty. My lips are so dry...

I crawl around on all fours, looking for the backpack. I take out the comb from the side pocket and start to do my hair. I don't need any light for that. Undo my braids, comb out my hair, braid it again, put in the barrettes—I could do all that in the pitch-dark at home when there was a power failure. I comb Lotte's hair and retie her ribbon. I'm sure the ribbon's all crumpled, but luckily she can't see it. Then it's Harald's and Rolfi's turn.

"I had to say my prayers all by myself last night," Lotte says reproachfully. "I've never had to do that before. Marta always prays with me, except when it's her day off."

What a morning—a morning of unrelieved darkness. We can't wash our faces or clean our teeth. Those things aren't essential to survival, but they're so important to feeling cheerful. I feel disgusting. Do I smell bad too?

I remember the broken glass and debris on the floor. I meant to sweep it up last night. If I do, I'll be able to let Rolfi crawl or toddle around in spite of the darkness. The most he'll do is bump into the walls and bruise himself.

I collect the blankets and drape them over the radiator, one on top of another. Erwin is still wrapped up in the fourth one.

As soon as I've talked with Herr Rockel, I'll sweep the floor thoroughly. The only thing is, where will I empty the dustpan?

Nine o'clock.

Herr Rockel should be calling anytime. I crouch down in front of the pipe and put my ear to it. I can hear Erwin breathing beside me.

Nothing yet. Maybe my watch is a little fast. Rolfi is whimpering. He's thirsty and hungry, I'm sure.

"I can't see to him now," I call to Harald and Lotte. "Herr Rockel will be here any moment!"

They hang onto Rolfi. He starts screaming and I clamp my ear to the pipe.

There he is at last.

"Hello?"

He has a deep voice. "Yes?" I say excitedly.

"So you're Gisela, the eldest?" he says. "I've got a daughter your age. My youngest child. Her name is Sophie. She's blonde, with long braids."

"I've got braids too, but they're brown."

"I picture you as her whenever I think of you kids," he says. "I think about you a lot. When your baby brother cries I can hear him faintly through the pipe."

He groans, but not the way a person groans when he's bored or tired. He must be in agony.

"It can't be easy for you," he goes on, "with three little brothers and a girl to look after. Even a grown woman would find it hard to cope. But you've every chance of getting out as long as you make yourselves heard, this morning especially. You need to shout as loud as you can—every fifteen minutes. They'll be searching for survivors everywhere today, especially in the air-raid shelters."

"Will you shout too?"

"No," he replies. "Most of this room is choked with rubble. No sound would get out."

That means we'll have to shout for him.

"Besides," he says with a sigh, "I need to save my strength. I can't use it up shouting. I'm feverish today. My leg is inflamed. The wound is filthy..."

"Does it hurt?" I asked—and could have slapped myself for asking such a silly question.

"I'm gritting my teeth," he replies. "But listen. Your brother told me you have some food with you. Ration it carefully. It may be a couple of days before they can dig you out, even if they hear you today. You've got to let them know you're here, that's the main thing, so shout as loud and as often as you can."

"It'll make us thirsty," I tell him, "and there's no water down here. We've only got two bottles with us. There's a little milk in one and the other's half-full of elderberry juice. That won't go far between five of us."

"But isn't there any water left in the tanks?" he asks, sounding surprised.

13

OF COURSE, THE TANKS ABOVE THE TOILETS! Why didn't we think of that before? Two big tanks full of water—maybe two gallons in each one! If we've got that much water...I could jump for joy!

Then I remember that Harald flushed the toilet just after the bomb hit. I remember hearing the water. Did someone else pull the chain after that? Yes, that's right, I did, but nothing happened.

I quickly think it through. Whenever you flush a toilet the tank fills up again, ready for the next flush. The tanks in our cubicles were full before the bomb landed, but the tank in the right-hand cubicle stayed empty after Harald pulled the chain.

What fools we are! We've robbed ourselves of half our precious water, purely from habit and because we didn't realize the seriousness of our situation right after the bomb.

Is the other tank empty too? One of us might have pulled the chain in the left-hand cubicle as well, and I've forgotten.

"Hello?" Rockel calls down the pipe. "Are you still there?"

"The tanks here may be empty," I sigh.

"That wouldn't be good. Take a look and let me know." I'm so wound up I hurry off in the wrong direction. I blunder into a wall, stumble on some debris, step back and listen.

"What are you doing, Gisel?" Harald calls.

Guided by the sound of his voice, I realize I must be in front of the broom closet. The first cubicle is to the left. I open the door. Phew, what a stink, but there's no way I'd flush now even if I could... Cautiously I climb on the seat, reach for the tank, lift the lid, and put my hand inside...

Nothing. It's completely empty. I can't feel any moisture even when I stand on my toes and feel the bottom with my fingertips. Of course, no water came out when I flushed this toilet myself.

I grope my way into the other cubicle. My hopes are drooping like a pricked balloon. I lower the lid, climb on it, feel for the tank and lift the lid. Then, holding my breath, I slowly insert my hand...

Water, water! The tank is full to the brim!

"It's full, the tank is full!" I cry exultantly. "We've got water— at least two gallons of—"

I break off. Have I woken Erwin? I listen, but there's no sound. He seems to be fast asleep, thank goodness.

So nobody flushed except Harald. Everyone after him must have used the right-hand toilet, probably for fear of stepping on something sharp. I jump down and hit my head on the cubicle door.

"Don't dare pull this chain, any of you!" I tell the others. "Use the right-hand cubicle only. The left-hand one is out of bounds!"

I grope my way back to the pipe. Rolfi is whining for milk, and Harald is complaining that he's hungry.

"Just one more minute," I say soothingly. I hit my shin on the pipe as I crouch down. It hurts like crazy.

"Hello?" I call. "One of our tanks is still full."

"That's good," I hear Rockel say. "But you must hoard it. It's no use just telling the others not to flush the toilet, they're too young. They might forget and pull the chain out of habit—or get the cubicles mixed up in the dark. You'd better lock the door."

That won't work, there isn't a key, and you can only bolt the door from inside.

Then I have a brainwave: all that debris on the floor! I explain my idea and Rockel approves. He says again how very important it is to make our water last. Washing? No, it's not necessary for survival. Drinking? Yes, but only in small quantities.

"Work out how much a day you can drink if you have to stay down here for a week."

"You mean it could take that long?" I exclaim in horror.

"Hope for the best," he says, "but always be prepared for the worst. And be sure to keep shouting. Start right now, and do it every fifteen minutes."

Of course, we need to call for help. I'd almost forgotten that, I'm so delighted about the water.

We agree to check in with each other every hour on the hour.

THERE'S LOTS TO DO NOW, which is good, because it'll help the time pass. I get the broom and a dustpan from the broom closet and sweep the whole room. It doesn't take long. I'm wide awake and less upset than I was, so I don't bump into things. I shovel all the debris and broken glass into the left-hand cubicle, where anyone going in by mistake will walk on it and know they're in the wrong place. That way, our water will be safe. It's disgusting, but we'll all have to use the toilet in the right-hand cubicle.

Next I take a rag from the broom closet and carefully go over the floor where the broken glass was to make sure I get every bit. Now Rolfi can toddle around on his own a bit without me worrying as much.

"Now it's breakfast time!" Harald calls.

Rolfi is sniveling and Lotte's begging for a drink.

"First we've got to shout 'Help!'" I say firmly. "Only those who shout as loud as they can will get breakfast."

I take Rolfi's hand and we shuffle over to the window shaft.

We're all quite used to the darkness by now, and we've got a pretty accurate picture of the room in our mind's eye. We know where the sink is, and the door, and the broom closet, and the pipe, and we can tell the cubicle side of the room from the door side and the sink side from the men's room side. It sounds different when we walk in different parts.

Harald gropes for my free hand, and I can feel Lotte holding onto my coat. We stop under the window shaft. I start shouting and Harald and Lotte join in.

"Help! Heeellp!"

But we don't make much noise without Erwin. He's got the loudest voice. The next time he'll have to shout too, no matter how tired he is. I can't believe we haven't woken him up with our racket. He must be completely exhausted. We yell "Help!" about twenty times before we have to give up. Harald says his mouth is too dry and Lotte complains that her throat hurts. I'm desperate for a drink.

I strain my eyes and ears. Maybe the shaft will suddenly be flooded with light. Maybe someone will call down: "It's all right, we'll have you out of there soon!" But the darkness and silence are as absolute as ever.

"You roared well, you pair of lions," I say. "Now we'll have something to eat."

"We have to wash our hands first," Lotte says sternly.

I suppose Marta drummed that into her. "Wash your hands before you eat, or a tummy-ache you'll get." Granny is always coming out with old-fashioned sayings like that. Mummy rolls her eyes impatiently sometimes when Granny isn't looking.

I can hear Harald waking Erwin. "Wake up! It's breakfast time!"

Erwin groans. I wait for him to protest—he only wanted to sleep, after all—but the mention of food gets his attention. I'd have had to wake him soon anyway, to join in calling for help. Fifteen minutes won't matter too much.

Lotte stubbornly insists on washing her hands. Erwin dismisses this as nonsense.

"You can only wash your hands if you've got water," he says. "We don't have any, so that's that."

"But we do!" we shout in chorus. I tell Erwin about my discovery, which astonishes him.

"Yes," I say. "We've got about two gallons."

"In that case," he says, "we really can wash our hands. Mine are all sticky."

"You see?" says Lotte. "Erwin thinks so too."

I think about what Herr Rockel said, but we've got a good amount of water now. Surely we could spare a tiny bit for washing. We'll use the smallest possible amount and we'll all use the same water. I insert the plug in the sink. We've even got two little towels in the backpack—terry towels, I can tell by the feel. Everyone wants to help as I climb over the pile of debris in the left-hand cubicle and onto the toilet seat armed with a mug and the bucket from the broom closet. I scoop out a mugful of water, then empty the bucket into the sink. We start by washing our faces. Rolfi, who gets his face washed by me, protests just like he does every morning.

It's not a real wash, because we can only wet our fingers in the water and run them over our eyes, lips and noses, leaning over the sink so we don't waste a drop. The next time around, we all wash our hands in the same water, with soap. Lotte complains that her cuffs have got wet. I wring them out as best I can and spread the wet towel to dry on the ice-cold radiator.

"If we've got as much water as this," says Lotte, "can we give some to the man next door?"

I leave Lotte's question unanswered. There's no way for us to get the water to Herr Rockel, and the more I think about it, the more I realize that less than two gallons among five people is very little, especially if we're trapped here for several days. Granny once said of a hard-hearted old woman: "The older they are, the colder they get." I'm almost nine years older than Lotte. I think I've grown "colder."

Erwin must have learned something about hygiene in school. "Is the water drinkable? I mean, are the tanks clean inside?"

I don't know, but we don't have any choice.

I decide to top up the milk and elderberry juice with water. They'll be very diluted, but at least they'll taste of *something*. I climb back on the toilet and Erwin hands me one of the bottles and the mug. I dip the mug in the water and pour into the bottle until I think it's full. Now everyone can have a mouthful of diluted elderberry juice—two mouthfuls, in fact.

Next I fill the milk bottle the same way—it's reserved for Rolfi. He's too young to drink from the bottle, so I try pouring him half a mug. I have to listen very carefully and check the level with my finger, because the neck of the bottle is so narrow that pouring some back in the dark would be almost impossible. Rolfi doesn't like his watery milk, and I can only get him to drink half of what I've poured. Then I let the others drink the rest, a small mouthful each.

There's only one sandwich for everyone again, plus I manage to find a plain bread and butter sandwich Mummy made for Rolfi, and break it up for him. It's terrifying to think that we may be trapped here for a whole week! I put my sandwich back in the bag, deciding I can hold out till this evening. When I announce that our next meal won't be till then, Erwin sighs but doesn't say anything. I hear him chewing, but that's all. Lotte reminds me of the cookies in my overcoat pocket.

I'd completely forgotten about them. I empty the crumbs and broken cookies from my pocket into an empty sandwich wrapper.

Harald flatly rebels. "I'm *so* hungry," he says reproachfully, "and you won't give me anything, you greedy thing! If Mummy knew, she'd—"

"If Mummy was here with us," Erwin breaks in, coming to my rescue, "and all we had was a few sandwiches, she wouldn't give you any more to eat than Gisel."

"Well," Harald grouches, "it'll be her fault if I starve to death."

"You don't starve to death as quickly as that," I tell him. "It takes time."

"How much time?" Lotte asks.

I don't know, not exactly. Ten days? Two weeks? Maybe even three weeks or longer?

"I read a book once," Erwin says, "about some shipwrecked sailors who ran out of food. They wound up eating one another."

"That's enough of that, Erwin!" I say sharply.

"Marta told me a story about a cannibal," Lotte chimes in. "It was so scary. Two children got lost in a forest at night. Then they saw the windows of a cottage through the trees and knocked on the door. A woman opened it and gave them something to eat. Her husband was a cannibal, but she didn't want them to get eaten, so she hid them before he came home. He kept roaming around the house, sniffing the air and saying: 'I can smell human flesh.' But he didn't find them. He went to bed and snored all night. Early the next morning his wife gave the children some breakfast and sent them off before the cannibal woke up. I couldn't help crying because it was so scary. Mummy asked why I was crying and I said Marta had told me the story. She got really mad at Marta, then she got dressed up and went out, and Marta got me ready for bed, and we both cried, but I wasn't crying about the children in the cannibal's cottage any more. It was because I felt so sorry for Mar—"

Ssh! A sound from outside our little circle! We all listen hard. The others even stop chewing.

"It's coming from that corner," Erwin whispers.

"Which corner?" Harald asks in a low voice.

"Over by the pipe…"

I glance at the luminous dial on my wristwatch. Ten past ten! I make my way over to the wall, grope for the pipe, and call: "Hello!"

"Did you forget the time?" I hear Herr Rockel reply. His voice sounds quite faint.

"We were having something to eat," I tell him, feeling guilty.

"Ah, that explains it. Are you being careful with your water?"

"Oh yes, we only used a mugful to wash in."

"You can't even do that!" He sounds shocked. "You have to stop washing completely. Dirt isn't nice, but thirst can be fatal. And you've only called for help once since the last time we spoke. If no one hears you, it will be just as fatal. They won't dig if they think there's no one left alive down here. It's very possible that you could all die a slow, miserable death, one after another. What if you died first and they were left alone in the dark, crying for help? I know that sounds brutal, Gisela, but your lives are hanging by a thread. I don't think you've really grasped that yet…"

I feel ashamed that I forgot the time. But there was so much that needed to be done quickly. He's right, though. Our situation is deadly serious.

"Soon you may be the oldest person left alive down here," he says next. "I know it must be hard, but you'll have to be more responsible, and…"

He breaks off, interrupted by a fit of coughing. It sounds awful, as if he's going to cough his lungs up!

"Have you caught a cold?" I ask hesitantly, when he finally stops.

"If only that was all," he replies with a bitter laugh. "It's this leg, and the cold, and lying here on the bare tiles. I've got a high temperature, but my head is clear—for how much longer, I don't know. I'm tough, though. Now, don't waste any more time. Shout, all of you! It'll keep you warm and it's your only hope. Mine too, because you'll be shouting for my sake as well..."

We agree to speak again at eleven.

14

Poor Herr Rockel is utterly dependent on us. If we don't attract attention very soon, he'll probably die. He needs medical treatment urgently, that's for sure.

The young ones are squealing with laughter. I can hear Lotte counting.

"If you're looking for Rolfi," Erwin says, "he's asleep on my lap."

He asks how Rockel is. I explain that his only hope is to get to a hospital as soon as possible. We've got to shout loudly—every fifteen minutes, till someone hears.

Erwin heaves a sigh. "There goes my sleep again," he says wearily.

I call Harald and Lotte.

"We were playing a great game of hide-and-seek," Harald grumbles.

Hide-and-seek? In the dark? How does it work?

Lotte explains. One person counts up to ten while the others hide. Then the one who was counting has to find the ones who are hiding. They might be anywhere—they're invisible, after all. The seeker needs a good sense of direction and hearing, because the people hiding will make a noise if they move.

"You play too!" Harald insists.

All right, it'll pass the time and warm us up. But first we need to call for help. I take Rolfi from Erwin so that he can get to his feet. Rolfi's heavy when he's asleep. We all crowd under the window shaft and shout. Rolfi wakes up with the racket, but that doesn't matter. He starts bawling, which adds to the volume, and I hug him tightly.

"Louder!" I call.

We shout till Erwin is too hoarse to go on. Then we stand with our heads tilted back, listening in the dark and hoping for a response: the sound of someone knocking or scraping debris away, or an answering voice...

Nothing. Just the rustle of silence and our own breathing.

"We'll do some more shouting in fifteen minutes," I say. "Till then, Erwin, you can doze while I play hide-and-seek with the others."

By now, I notice, the younger ones can move around the room almost as easily as they would in daylight. Lotte gives me a push.

"You stand in corner number 3 and count up to ten," she tells me. "Then you come looking for us. Erwin, lie down inside the broom closet or you'll get in our way."

I hear the door of the closet close. Corner number 3? Where's that?

I discover that Harald and Lotte have assigned numbers to the four corners of the room. The one beside the broom closet is number 1, the one beside the pipe is number 2, the sink corner is number 3, and the one under the window shaft is number 4. I memorize this arrangement. Before long I'm standing beside the sink in corner number 3, counting up to ten. I'll let the kids play for as long as possible, it'll distract them. They won't notice their hunger and thirst so much.

I actually enjoy the game, even though I'm too old for such things. You have to keep your ears pricked if you want to win. If you're hiding, you have to pick up your feet and control your breathing, and not bump into anything. That will make a noise and betray where you are—or where you were a moment ago.

I'm lucky enough to catch Harald. He counts up to ten while Lotte and I sneak off and hide. The fifteen minutes pass very quickly.

"That's it!" I call. "Time for more shouting!"

"Already?" Harald protests.

I haul Erwin out of the broom closet. "Just when I was dozing off," he sighs.

Once more we holler for help until we run out of breath, and once more we listen in vain. Then Erwin heads to the broom closet again and we go on playing hide-and-seek. I keep looking at my watch until it's time to speak with Herr Rockel again.

"I heard you all shouting," he says.

"We shouted 'Help!' twenty times each time," I tell him. "Now we're completely hoarse."

"It's lucky there's air coming in from somewhere. If there wasn't..." He's racked by another fit of coughing and has to fight for breath before he can go on. "If there wasn't, we'd be unconscious by now. Or dead."

A shiver runs down my spine. It hadn't occurred to me

before that we could be short of air. How lucky we are, in spite of everything!

"I'm glad you're there," Rockel says. "I keep trying to listen, but it's an effort for me to lift my head to the pipe, and it's getting harder all the time. Still, it takes my mind off things. It's so nice to hear you laughing..."

"That was the younger ones playing hide-and-seek," I tell him. "I'm not in the mood, but it's keeping them busy."

I don't think he heard me, because he says: "It reminds me of my own children at that age..." And after a long minute, when I think he's moved away from the pipe, I hear him say, "Try to make them laugh often, all right?"

I slowly straighten up. Will he be able to reach the pipe an hour from now, at noon? I wonder what he looks like. Short and dark-haired and sturdy like Daddy, or tall and thin like Grandpa Häusler?

He's a father, whatever he looks like, and it's lucky for us he's here. He's given us some very useful advice.

I peer at my watch. The time hustles us from one activity to the other: shouting "Help!" and playing hide-and-seek. For Erwin that means dozing off and waking up every fifteen minutes. But our voices are becoming hoarser. All this shouting has exhausted us. The younger ones go on strike.

I have to threaten not to play with them any more unless they help to shout.

Back home I could go to my room if I wanted to be alone for a while. Down here I can't be alone—can't even think my own thoughts. Someone's always asking me something. I can't leave the younger kids on their own, now that I've taken Mummy's place. They don't realize that I need a little time to myself—that I need to recharge my batteries. All they want me to do is play with them.

Time for the next shouting session. We gather in corner number 4 and yell till we're hoarse.

"I've got an idea," Erwin says breathlessly. "Maybe they'll hear *this* better..." He gropes his way to the broom closet. All at once he calls: "Don't be scared, all of you, I'm going to make a racket!" And he does—by banging the dustpan against one of the cubicle doors. It makes much more noise than banging it against the wall.

I give Rolfi to Lotte to hold and hammer on the other cubicle door with my shoe. Surely they'll hear it up there?

We pause to listen. The younger ones keep still.

Nothing.

IT'S TWELVE O'CLOCK ALREADY. Time to check with Herr Rockel. "Hello?" I call hoarsely. Rockel answers. I'm relieved he can still reach the pipe.

But I can barely make out what he's saying, his voice is so feeble and husky.

"I'm absolutely parched," he says with an effort. "It's the fever."

What am I to say? I can't do anything to help. For lack of a better idea, I ask him the name of his youngest daughter, the one who's my age. He did tell me her name before, but I've forgotten it.

"Sophie," he says wearily.

My question seems to have depressed him. I'm still wondering how to cheer him up a bit when he says: "That banging of yours was good and loud. Let's hope they heard you up there..."

"No sign of that yet," I say sadly.

He mutters something, but so quietly that I only catch a word or two: "It'll soon...be too late."

"What did you say?" I ask him, appalled.

He clears his throat. Then, in an entirely different, more cheerful tone, he says, "We'll stick it out, won't we? We won't give in."

No, we won't give in. I think of Mummy and Daddy. They would try to keep my spirits up if they were next door and unable to reach us. "Stick it out, Gisel," they'd call. "Whatever you do, don't give in!"

He has another awful coughing fit. Picturing how tormented with thirst he must be, I think of our bottle of elderberry juice. What if we could give him a little of it?

But then, what if Rolfi died of thirst and Herr Rockel survived? In any case, how would we get it to him? There's no point thinking about it.

"It's time for more shouting," I tell him. "We'll shout and bang on the doors. I'll come back here at one o'clock."

"Listen for sounds in between," he says, the breath rasping in his throat. "Sounds from overhead..."

It'll soon be too late...Will he die a lonely, terrible death before they reach us? He's still hoping we'll be heard. But, even if a rescue team does hear us, it'll be a while before they can dig us out. Herr Rockel needs help right *now*!

It'll soon be too late...That reminds me of Grandpa Karl's slow death. But he had lots of nursing and attention. He lay in bed with Granny waiting on him day and night. She wasn't teaching then, and the war wasn't going nearly so badly. Dr Schulz came whenever she called him. So did we kids, when Grandpa wanted to see us. We played chess only a few days before he died, he and I, with his lovely little hand-carved chessmen.

Daddy got a week's compassionate leave, so that he could see his father for the last time. Grandpa seemed to have been waiting for him. On the morning of the day he died he asked quietly, "Is he here yet?" When Granny shook her head, he said, "It'll soon be too late..." Daddy arrived just before noon and Grandpa died a few hours later. We were all there: Granny, Daddy, Mummy, Harald, Erwin and I, all in our best Sunday clothes. He died very peacefully. I think we were far more upset than Grandpa was.

The whole village accompanied his coffin to the graveyard, and the veterans of the First World War turned out in his honour.

If we aren't back home by spring, his grave will be thick with weeds. That's a sad thought.

IT'S PAST NOON, but it's too soon to eat anything. I allow each of us a mouthful of diluted elderberry juice. This time I allow myself one too, because I've got to be able to call for help.

"But only one mouthful, and no cheating!" I tell the others. That goes for me too. Only Rolfi gets more, but not as much as the last time. I pour a little of the watery milk into his mug and he drinks it greedily. At least the milk isn't going bad, it's so cold down here.

"More!" he splutters.

No, no more, but it's all I can do to insist, he sobs so pathetically.

Lotte is crying too. I stroke her crumpled hair ribbon. "As soon as we're out of here," I say soothingly, "you can all eat and drink as much as you like."

"No, we can't," Erwin corrects me. "People who've almost died of hunger and thirst have to be careful not to overeat. They have to take it slowly or they burst their intestines. Our teacher told us that."

Can't Erwin stop saying things like this? I was only trying to cheer Lotte up.

"Once I'm out of here," Harald announces, "I'll eat and drink as much as I like, even if I do burst. I'll have beef stew with dumplings and roast pork and applesauce and waffles with strawberry jam and sausages and potatoes and—"

"Stop it!" I yell. "You're getting on my nerves!"

Now Harald's crying too. I rummage around in the food bag. Maybe there's been another miracle of the loaves and fishes—maybe the sandwiches we've already eaten have replaced themselves…

Nonsense, that's just wishful thinking. There are only two sandwiches left. That's only half a sandwich apiece, plus there's the one I didn't eat this morning. I really should have only given out half sandwiches this morning, but everyone's complaining of hunger as it is. I also count five apples by touch. I know what they taste like, and that they're red on one side and yellow on the other, because they come from the apple tree behind our barn. I also know the taste of the sausages, a string of six. They're pork sausages from the last time the Häuslers slaughtered a pig. And six hard-boiled eggs from our seven hens. Oh yes, and there's the wrapper full of broken cookies. My stomach is knotted with hunger. I quickly zip up the bag. We might be down here for a week. Or even longer...

15

TIME TO MAKE A RACKET AGAIN. We gather in corner number 4. Our voices sound quite different this time—lubricated, I guess. What a difference a mouthful of watery elderberry juice makes, even if it hardly tastes of elderberry any more. But we only manage eleven calls for help because we quickly become hoarse again. Erwin bangs on the cubicle door a few times with the dustpan.

"Come and play," I say wearily. "And you, Erwin, grab half an hour's sleep. I'll do the banging next time."

But the younger ones are tired of hide-and-seek and want me to tell them a story. How about The Wolf and the Seven Little Goats? No, they don't want that one because they already know it. Mummy must have read it to Harald, just as she read it to Erwin and me in the old days, and Lotte has heard it from Marta.

My long-time favorite was The Little Mermaid, but that's probably too long for six- and seven-year-olds. Too sad, besides. Nearly all the other stories that I think of mention food, which rules them out. Finally I come up with The Fisherman and His Wife. I've heard it so often from Granny, I could tell it in my sleep. Harald doesn't know the story. Lotte does, but she wants to hear it again.

They both listen closely. I'm interrupted only once by Lotte, who complains that she's cold.

"Snuggle up against me," I tell her. She does, and I tell the story to the end, when the fisherman's wife, not satisfied with all the wishes she's been granted by the flounder whose life her husband has spared, which is really a prince with magical powers, says she wants to be like God:

"'Go home,' the flounder tells the fisherman. 'Your wife is back in your hovel again.' And there they still live to this day..."

The room falls silent. I can't hear a sound from Erwin, only from Rolfi, who lets out an occasional sigh. He's too young to have understood the story, but something else has his full attention: my wristwatch. He's fiddling with it now, tugging at the strap and giving impatient little grunts. I won't stop him, it'll keep him occupied.

Then Lotte says, "Won't Herr Rockel die unless he has something to eat? Can't we at least give him something to drink?" she pleads. "We've got a whole tank full of water."

"How?" I ask her impatiently. "Through the wall?"

Erwin isn't asleep. "There's the pipe," he says slowly. "Water would run through it. We'd just have to be careful not to spill any when we were pouring it in."

"But it would run down the wall on the other side."

"Not if he put his mouth around the pipe."

Erwin is good at "practicalities," as Grandpa Häusler calls them. A moment later he's over by the pipe. I can picture exactly what he's doing, although I can't see him: cupping his hand under the pipe and nodding to himself. Then I hear him calling Herr Rockel.

His third "Hello!" seems to do the trick. "We're going to send you something to drink!" he calls. "Put the end of the pipe in your mouth as soon as you hear me whistle!"

Harald and Lotte head toward the pipe. Erwin is rummaging in the food bag. "Which bottle shall I take," he calls in my direction, "elderberry or milk?"

"The elderberry juice. The milk is for Rolfi."

I hear a rustle, then a whistle, then a soft gurgling sound. Erwin is pouring some juice into the pipe. I hold my breath. After all, he can't see what he's doing!

"Don't mention it," I hear him call. "I'm sorry we can't spare much, but..."

He seems to be listening again. Then: "Yes, we will," he calls. "Goodbye till the next time!"

"What did he say?" Lotte asks.

"Did he say thank you?" asks Harald.

"You bet! He sends his thanks to everyone and says we have to keep shouting and making a racket as often as possible."

Lotte heaves a contented sigh. "He'll feel much better now."

It's all very well for them to feel so pleased; they aren't in charge of our meager supplies like I am. I wanted Herr Rockel to have a drink, but I can't help thinking that now there'll be less for all of us, and if we're trapped for days, we'll run out of water.

Rolfi is struggling to get away from me and join the others beside the pipe. I let him go and listen to him crawling over there. He doesn't feel safe walking by himself in the dark, I expect. Now all four of them are together and I'm here by myself—alone with my responsibilities. Responsibilities! I'm starting to hate that word!

I get to my feet. As I do so, something goes crack under my shoe. I bend down to investigate—and a shiver of horror runs through me: it's my watch, I've stepped on my watch! Hurriedly, I pick it up in the hope that it might still be going. But the glass is smashed and I can feel that one of the hands has come off. I hold it to my ear and shake it hard. No use. I go cold all over—even colder than I was before—and hurl it at the floor in disgust.

Rolfi must have managed to get it off my coat. The narrow strap was pretty worn, or did he unbuckle it? But it's pointless to wonder how it happened. The fact is, we won't know what time it is any more, won't have a clue whether it's morning or afternoon, night or day.

Anyway, I know it's time to call for help again. I get the dustpan from the broom closet and bang on the cubicle door as hard as I can. I vent all my anger and misery on the door as if it were to blame for everything. Why, oh why, oh why has this happened to us?

"Gisel!" I hear Erwin shout from somewhere behind me. "You'll wear yourself out! Let me take over!"

I lower the dustpan. "I've smashed my watch," I tell him mournfully. "I stepped on it."

Why should I put the blame on Rolfi? I allowed him to play with the thing and now it's broken. Tears spring to my eyes. I toss the dustpan into the broom closet and crouch down in front of it. I'm ready to burst into tears, but the children would hear. I must control myself. Granny often talks about "self-control"—another of the words I detest. Self-control makes you look different on the outside than what you feel inside. Down here I have to hide my true feelings; otherwise Erwin and the others would lose hope.

"Gisel?" It's Erwin. He gropes for my hand and crouches down beside me. "Rockel has got a watch too," he says gently.

That's true, he has! That means we won't be completely ignorant of the time.

"Still," I say, "soon he might be past telling us what time it is."

"We gave him something to drink, don't forget."

"How much?"

"About a quarter of a mugful, I guess. I heard him swallow four or five times."

Now I'm sorry we didn't give him more.

Erwin's attempt to comfort me has helped. I'm feeling more hopeful again.

But now Rolfi's crying. Of course, I should have changed him ages ago. He'll be sore, on top of being hungry. With all the shouting, I've forgotten to hold him over the toilet this morning, like I meant to. I call him. He starts to feel his way along the wall, then suddenly stops.

"Come here, Rolfi!" I call.

But he doesn't. What's he up to? He can't be more than a few steps away, so I crawl toward him. He's sitting on the floor, playing with the pieces of my watch! If he puts a piece in his mouth...I quickly pick him up. He screams and kicks, wanting to be put down. That's all we need: Rolfi choking on a bit of my broken watch!

Time to change his diaper. I feel for the backpack.

"I heard someone knocking!" Harald cries suddenly.

I listen. We all listen. Rolfi is whining and sniveling.

"Hush, Rolfi!"

Now it's as quiet as the grave. Not a sound.

"But I heard it," Harald insists. "Really, I did!"

"Maybe it was your heart thumping," says Lotte.

We get back to business. Erwin crawls around on the tiles, gathering up the pieces of my watch. Rolfi can't get his hands on a single bit, Erwin knows that as well as I do. I take off Rolfi's dirty diaper, clean him up, smear his bottom with ointment and bundle him up again. The dirty diaper goes behind the toilet bowl.

"Will you tell us another story, Gisel?" Harald asks.

Isn't it time to call for help again? It won't hurt to make noise more often. I hammer on the cubicle door with the dustpan and everyone shouts, then we listen.

All at once we really do hear a noise above us. And again! And again! It sounds like a woodpecker a little way off. Then silence.

"They're waiting for us to answer," Erwin whispers. "We have to make a noise!"

I grab the dustpan again and we yell like mad, although we're all hoarse. I shout "Help!" as loud as I can, five or six times. That should do it. Now we listen again. Will they answer, or did we only imagine that someone was knocking because we've wished for it so much?

There it is, even louder than before.

"Now let's try the dustpan again," Erwin whispers. He takes it from me and hammers on the cubicle door.

They reply.

I pick Rolfi up and give him a big hug. Then I let him slide to the floor and hug Harald and Lotte. We're saved! The searchers have found us—they know we're down here! Erwin and I hug each other too. I almost can't believe how lucky we are! My eyes prick with tears, and I realize how frightened I've been that no one would find us. A great feeling of relief surges through me.

It doesn't matter now if we don't know what time it is. Soon we'll be outside again, outside in the daylight with Granny. And Lotte will be with—who? Marta or her Mummy?

16

THE KNOCKING HAS STOPPED. Of course, now they'll have to start digging. There must be a mountain of rubble on top of the toilets. It'll take them a while to clear away enough to get us out.

I haven't told Herr Rockel yet. He'll be so glad, and it will help him to hold on till we're rescued.

I give Rolfi to Erwin and grope my way over to the end of the pipe.

"Hello!" I call.

I hear a groan. Then faintly, "Yes?"

"It's me, Gisel. They were knocking! They've heard us!"

"Thank God," I hear him mutter. Then, after a short pause: "Keep answering. Use a broom handle—knock on the ceiling so they know you're still alive. And don't eat up the food you've got left. Ration it carefully, and your water too. It could take hours still..."

I ask how he is.

"Not good." He groans again. "My leg...it hurts like the devil, and it's so cold..."

"We'll pour some more water down the pipe," I tell him.

I can afford to be generous now. Soon we'll be able to drink as much as we like!

I call Erwin while I'm searching for the bag and almost trip over it outside the broom closet. I hear him give Rolfi to Lotte and Harald. I fish the elderberry bottle out of the bag and fill it quickly from the tank.

"Hello!" I call down the pipe. "We've got the water for you!"

All I hear is a groan, then a grating sound. His teeth against the metal?

"Go on," I whisper to Erwin. "You're the expert."

He whistles, then pours some water into the pipe.

I wait a moment, then bend down. "Hello?" I call. "Did you get it all right?"

I hear a groan and some labored breathing. Then: "I couldn't keep my mouth over the pipe..."

"Never mind," I try to comfort him. "They'll have you out of there soon, and then you'll get something to drink. Coffee or tea, maybe. Something nicer than water from an old tank, anyway."

He says something, but so faintly that the only word I catch is "sleep." I'm about to stand up when he says something else: "When the war's over, you must go and see Sophie...No. 14 Ro... Oldenburg..."

"*What* street?" I call back. "I didn't get that!"

But he doesn't speak again. All I can hear is his feverish breathing. He's fallen asleep, maybe. I make a mental note to ask him the name of the street in Oldenburg the next time we talk.

Then I realize I forgot to ask him what time it is. Oh well, next time. An hour from now.

But we won't know when an hour has gone by. All right, when we *think* an hour has gone by.

I'm shivering with cold all of a sudden.

"SURELY WE CAN have something to eat *now*, Gisel?" Harald says loudly.

I decide to treat us to some food in spite of Herr Rockel's warnings: half a sandwich and one sausage each. I hear the others clustering around me. We all sit on the floor in corner number 1, in front of the broom closet.

The others can hardly wait for me to find the little kitchen knife and cut up the string of sausages. I can hardly wait myself, since I still haven't eaten anything today! I sniff them. They still smell good. At least that's one advantage of the cold down here.

We're all quiet as we chomp away, and Rolfi happily eats a quarter of the sandwich I'd saved from this morning. They're all grateful when I let them have a mouthful of water from the bottle.

"I'd think we could have two mouthfuls," Erwin says, "since we'll be out of here before long."

I agree to this.

"I like lemonade better than water," says Lotte.

"And I like cocoa better," Harald chimes in.

We finish our lunch in no time.

"I'm full up now," Harald announces with a sigh. I'm sure he's holding his tummy. He always does when he says that.

"Me too," says Lotte. "I won't need anything more to eat for a long, long time."

I can't help grinning. Lotte can't see me, luckily. How long is "a long, long time"? She'll be hungry again in a few hours, but that won't be my problem any more. In a few hours we're bound to be up in the light of day, in the warmth, with plates of steaming food in front of us.

"Now you can have a sleep," I tell Erwin.

"Now?" he exclaims. "What, just when it's getting exciting? I couldn't possibly!"

More knocking overhead. It seems louder than the last time. Erwin gets the broom and bangs on the ceiling. Before long, the signals from above and below fall into the same rhythm: three taps from the surface are answered by three from the cellar.

This goes on for quite a while. Then the people on the surface break off. They know we're in a fit state to signal. Now they have to get to digging. We keep listening for sounds overhead. Can we hear the rumble of debris being cleared away? The scrape of shovels? The rattle of a pneumatic drill? Voices? Shouting?

Nothing.

Harald and Lotte are romping around in the dark, and so is Rolfi. It sounds as if they're holding hands with him in the middle. Every few minutes they ask me when the men are coming to get us.

"Soon" is all I can tell them, over and over, because I have no idea of the time. It must be late afternoon, maybe three or even four o'clock. That would mean we've been trapped down here for a full twenty-four hours.

It'll be dark outside soon. Or is it dark already? Maybe our excitement has made the time pass faster.

Maybe Granny herself is up there helping to clear away the rubble. Will we manage to get to Dresden tonight? If we do, I'll be able to celebrate my birthday there tomorrow, as if none of this had happened.

I can't help thinking of Herr Rockel. Oldenburg...That's in the far northwest—right at the other end of Germany. I've never been there.

I have to remember to ask him the name of the street, although Mummy or Granny would probably be able to find his address by asking at Oldenburg's town hall. But we won't have to do that. Herr Rockel will be brought to the surface like us, through a hole in his ceiling or a hole in the wall between us. Then he'll be nursed back to health at a hospital, and after that he'll be able to go back to Oldenburg—to his wife and his daughter Sophie, who live at No. 14 in a street with a name that starts with "Ro."

Is he still asleep? Should I call him? His leg hurts so much when he's awake. I think I should let him sleep for now. It'll be noisy enough when the rescuers get closer. Let him rest while he can!

I'm sleepy too, but I can't give in to it; I have to stay awake. Granny once said the best remedy for tiredness is hard work. But what can I do down here?

I could tidy up the backpack and the food bag, for one thing. Let's hope it'll warm me up. All these layers of clothing aren't much help. A hot drink or a bowl of soup would keep the cold out.

They're knocking again. Louder now.

"Come in!" Erwin calls.

He must have woken up in the middle of a dream. I hear him

jump to his feet and pick up the broom. The rhythm of the signals has changed: four taps—pause; four taps—pause. Maybe they want to check how alert we are. Well, at least we can still count up to four!

Erwin bangs the ceiling with the broomstick four times, then four times more. A hush has fallen in here. Harald and Lotte are listening intently. I sense that even Rolfi seems to have pricked up his ears.

Another exchange of signals, then silence.

"Hey, Gisel," Erwin says excitedly, "I've got something in my eye, plaster or something. It must have come from up there. Maybe our ceiling vibrates whenever they hit a chunk of concrete with their poles, or whatever they use to signal with. It must mean they're getting closer."

Maybe, maybe not.

"*Are* they getting closer?" Lotte asks.

"Much closer," I say firmly, as if I'm God almighty and know all the answers.

More than an hour must have gone by since we first heard them knocking. I'd imagined that they would be within calling distance by now, but I realize it's going to take a lot longer. Will we have to spend another whole night down here?

ERWIN HAS GONE BACK TO SLEEP. At least, he hasn't said anything for a while. Unlike him, the younger ones are being noisy and whiny.

"I'm so bored!" Harald says plaintively.

I suggest playing a game of ghosts. This involves flitting around the room on tiptoe, making ghoulish noises. But Rolfi, who doesn't recognize our eerie voices, screams with terror.

What about a fairy tale? No, they've got to keep moving, not sit there on the tiled floor getting even colder. So I invent a game that will work in here. They gather around me and I tell them a story. If I say the word "black," they all have to fall over backward. If I say "white," they have to jump to their feet.

It works, though not with Rolfi. He has no idea whether to fall over or stand up. As for Harald, he simply sits there. He roars with laughter when we finally discover this. Lotte is indignant.

"You stay sitting down too," he tells her, giggling.

I send a silent prayer to our rescuers: Please, please get to us soon! I can't keep this bunch in good spirits much longer.

MORE KNOCKING, a little louder now. Erwin signals back. Is this going to go on all night? I feel sorry for Erwin. Fast asleep, yet he wakes up every time. I'm surprised he's roused by such a relatively faint sound. I doubt that it would wake *me* once I was fast asleep.

Poor Erwin, you deserve a night's rest. I'll take over for you.

We sit on the floor making animal noises and getting the others to guess what we are. Lotte finds this game too childish—she gets it right every time, even when I hiss like a snake. Next we dance around the room in a chain. Then we take the top blanket from the radiator, spread it out on the floor, and take turns doing somersaults. Lotte finds the floor too hard, but Rolfi rolls over sideways, giggling.

I hold Harald and Lotte by the ankles and make them walk on their hands. Wheelbarrows, we call it. This keeps them amused for a while, but only until they bump into the walls and bruise themselves.

At last they're sleepy. I send them in to use the right-hand toilet. As soon as they've finished I change Rolfi's diaper. I fold one of the blankets in half for Harald and Lotte to lie on. Another one will be a cover for them. The third blanket, which is still lying on the floor, will be for Rolfi and me.

I find some things to use as pillows: two hand towels for Rolfi, Granny's cardigan for Lotte, and the folded backpack for Harald. Erwin can rest his head on the food bag, which isn't full anymore. As for me, I'll be staying awake.

"Want something to eat before bedtime?" I ask.

Of course they do. I give them a choice between apples and boiled eggs. Harald wants an apple, Lotte an egg. She almost snatches it from my hand when I peel it for her and hold it out.

"There's no salt," she complains.

Sometimes Lotte would try the patience of a saint. I hide my annoyance and rummage in the bag feeling for the salt shaker. I've managed to drop the pieces of eggshell into the bag.

"I can't find the salt," I tell Lotte. "If you don't want the egg without salt, I'll eat it."

No answer. She's already munching away, I can hear. I peel another egg for Rolfi. When he's done, I eat the rest of the sandwich I'd saved from breakfast. The bread is dry around the edges, but it tastes wonderful!

"Now I'd like an apple," Lotte says with her mouth full. After that, she has the nerve to ask for another egg!

That's enough, I tell them. We have to save some food for tomorrow, even though I expect they'll reach us during the night. But Herr Rockel said we should always be prepared for the worst. At the moment I can't imagine anything worse than having to wait till tomorrow—my birthday!

Finally, everyone gets a drink of water and a piece of cookie. Rolfi nibbles a cookie too. I dip it in his mug until it's soft, then finish the water myself.

I put the children to bed.

"Rolfi must lie between us again," Lotte says.

Harald wants his brother with him too, so I lay Rolfi down in the middle and tuck them in. I spread my blanket beside them. I want to be near enough to pull the blanket over them if it slips off.

I've settled them down at long last.

But, just when I think they'll fall asleep, the knocking starts again. It doesn't sound as if our rescuers are any closer—in fact, they might not be any closer than the first time we heard them. Maybe it's just that they're signaling with something different?

Erwin has already got to his feet and is banging on the ceiling with the broomstick.

The poor boy must be thirsty. I bring him the bottle of water.

"How much can I drink?" he whispers.

"As much as you like. We'll be out of here soon."

He drinks greedily, draining the bottle.

"Do you want something to eat too?" I ask, but there's no reply. He's already back in the broom closet. I recognize the sound of the door closing.

Rolfi is asleep by the time I go back to Harald and Lotte, but they're both wide awake, thanks to all the banging.

Lotte demands a bedtime story. "Marta always tells me one at home."

"What about your Mummy?" I ask in surprise.

"She usually goes out at night."

I can't think of any stories. I'm feeling wrung out and empty-headed. But then I have an idea:

"*Once upon a time, four children and their mother and grandmother went on a long journey in the middle of winter. It was wartime. On the way, their mother suddenly had to leave them because she was going to have a baby. Not long afterward, while they were waiting in a railway station, some enemy bombers flew over. They lost sight of their grandmother in the confusion, which meant they were all on their own. To escape from the bombers they took refuge in an air-raid shelter. There they met a little girl who had also become separated from her mother—*"

"But that's me!" Lotte exclaims. "I already know that story! It's no fun!"

Harald agrees. He's still debating what sort of story he *does* want when Lotte whispers: "I haven't said my prayers yet."

"Say them, then."

"Marta always says them with me."

I get her to say the first words. It's a rhyming prayer I've never heard before.

"You can say them by yourself," I tell her. "You proved that last night. You're old enough at seven to say them without Marta."

"I always include Mummy and Marta."

"Not your Daddy?"

"He's dead. He was killed." She pauses, then whispers, "Would you like to be included too?"

"Yes. Pray for me and all of us down here. For now, we belong together."

"All right." She draws a deep breath. "And God bless Gisel, and Erwin, and Harald, and Rolfi. And Herr Rockel, because he's all alone in there behind that wall. And please make his temperature go down and make him not feel so cold."

I nod and stroke her hair.

"Should I pray for anyone else?"

"My parents and grandparents, maybe?"

"But I don't know them!"

I sigh. "You can pray for people you don't know, can't you?"

Yes, Lotte agrees that she can.

"Maybe you should include the people up above us, who are doing their best to get us out of here," I suggest. "They must be working very hard."

I hear her whispering.

"Finished," she says, sounding relieved.

I stroke her cheek. "Sleep well, little Lotte…"

"Same to you," she says softly. I can already hear her breathing peacefully.

"Lotte?" I whisper.

She doesn't answer.

17

HERR ROCKEL...I've been so busy with the children I haven't thought about him for a while. I wonder how he is. I shuffle over to the pipe and call "Hello?" Then I listen. All I can hear is his rapid, hoarse breathing. He sounds very sick, and no wonder, with a high temperature.

What time is it? Eight o'clock? Maybe nine or even ten? It must be pitch-dark outside by now, since it's winter. The streetlights are blacked out and there won't be any light escaping from windows. Anyone who lets light show could be punished severely. At home we pull black roller blinds down over the windows at dusk. They fit the windows perfectly, so nothing shows through but the tiniest chinks of light.

How wonderful it used to be when every window glowed, and the streetlights were so bright you could see people's faces!

Back then, in peacetime, I was a little girl like Lotte. A little girl who still liked playing with her dolls.

If it were peacetime...Yes, what would it be like? The news reporters would have nothing important enough to announce! There'd be no war office communiqués and no war reports of any kind. What would that leave? A few road accidents? A minor earthquake somewhere far away?

If it were peacetime, we would be at home, sitting around the table having supper by the glow of our lamp. The French clock on Daddy's desk would be ticking softly, and at seven the cuckoo would peep out of the clock on the wall and cuckoo seven times. Oh, and the table! The windmill-pattern plates—we left those behind too—would be piled with food, including several kinds of sausage, especially the liver sausage Daddy likes so much. There'd be slices of cold beef and tinned sardines and a bowl of bananas and oranges, and everyone could take as much butter as they liked, and Daddy would be planning a sleigh trip for next weekend. Where to? Maybe to the mountains we can see in the distance from our garden.

Those sleigh trips with Daddy were always so special. And maybe Mummy would say, "But first Gisel must have a new pair of winter boots; she's grown out of her old ones. We'll go shopping in town tomorrow..."

Or, depending on what time it is, Mummy would be washing the dishes and I'd be drying. And Daddy would be sitting at his desk—not in uniform, of course—getting ready for Monday morning. He was a teacher like Granny—he taught Latin to the senior class at the boys' school. His students were really young men already, not boys. And there wouldn't be any black crosses against their names in the school register, and Daddy would have no need to shake his head and mutter: "My God, not Bernhard Kornbrenner too! What a promising youngster he was..."

And if I was already in bed and had turned off the light, the moon might be shining into my room...

But it's wartime. Daddy is in uniform and far away, where it's very dangerous. Many of his former students have been killed, and no light must escape from the windows, and the moon can't shine in, and the table is empty, and we've had to leave our home and now we're here, buried beneath a mountain of rubble.

I'm the only one awake. My eyelids are heavy, but I can't go to sleep. I have to be able to answer any signals from our rescuers. I'll also have to look after Rolfi if he wakes up, and be ready to wake the others before the men break through the ceiling.

Now that everyone else is asleep, I feel wonderfully alone and more at peace. I haven't had a minute all day to think of Mummy and Daddy and home. I can picture our house and garden in the snow and see the two snowmen on either side of the garden gate, as tall and still as sentries. Erwin and his friends built them after Christmas, shouting and laughing loudly while they worked. Each snowman was armed with a twig broom and had a helmet made of folded newspaper. Most of the people who passed our house chuckled when they saw them.

I have a vision of Daddy sitting on the edge of a forest—a pine forest like the one behind the Häuslers' farmhouse. The snow is glittering in the sun, the sky is bright blue.

Daddy is all alone. Perhaps he has only gone to the edge of the forest for a look at the snowy countryside. He's in uniform, sitting in the snow with his back against a tree. His rifle is lying beside him and his eyes are shut. I suspect he's thinking about us. Maybe he just received a letter from home. Mummy writes him a letter every week, and I write to him fairly often too.

I love you so much, Daddy. I want to give you a hug. Can't you see me? Why don't you get up?

I walk over to him, the snow crunching under my feet. Hasn't he heard me? I bend over. My shadow falls across him, but he still doesn't look up. He must be lost in thought. Maybe he's having a nap. But...sitting on this cold snow?

"Daddy!" I whisper.

No response. His head is tilted at a slight angle, his eyes are shut. He must be asleep, so I won't disturb him. I'm sure he's just had a hard day's fighting. I decide to go for a walk through the trees—only for a little way, so I don't lose sight of the edge of the forest. I keep turning to look at Daddy with his back against the tree.

I come to a small clearing. There's an oak tree in the center. Some of its branches have things dangling from them. Old rags hung out to dry?

Going nearer, I'm horrified to discover what's hanging there. Five human beings: a woman and four men—no, two of them are youngsters. Their hands are tied behind their backs. One of the boys, who can't be any older than me, is staring at me with his eyes open. I can't bear it—I go cold all over.

Suddenly his eyes move. He's laughing at me. He clears his throat and coughs. He's alive, no doubt about it!

Overcome with confusion, I try to collect my thoughts. I must cut the boy down, but how? I don't have a ladder or a knife to sever the rope.

Daddy! He can help. I hurry back to the edge of the forest, threading my way between the trees, and look around. Daddy isn't there anymore. All I can see are his tracks. There's a big red patch in the snow where he was sitting.

It's blood! Daddy was sitting in a pool of blood and I didn't notice! Why didn't I speak louder? Why didn't I touch him, give him a hug? Then I'd have known what was wrong—I could have gone for help. Or was he already dead? Who killed him—the partisans?

Oh, Daddy!

I WAKE UP WITH A START, furious with myself for having dozed off. What an awful nightmare that was! I shake my head to try and clear it and tell myself it was only a dream.

I've had enough of this darkness and fear. Tomorrow is going to be a *good* day. I'm so glad they'll get us out of here in a few more hours. I want to believe that we'll go home again, and that everything will be the way we left it, even if the Russians did occupy our village. They don't really have faces like the one on the poster. That was just meant to fool us into fighting even harder to defeat them. They won't smash Mummy's best dinner dishes or play football with my doll or throw Harald's teddy into the fire.

And when the snow has melted, or maybe when the lilac is in bloom, we'll go home. Daddy may have got there before us, so he'll be waiting at the garden gate with Bella. And he'll take Mummy in his arms and swing her around—no, she'll be holding the baby, so he'll bend down and kiss Mummy on the lips. And then he'll toss Rolfi, Harald and Erwin into the air and catch them, one after the other, and give me a big hug and pull my braids, while Bella romps around and jumps up and licks our faces, beside herself with joy.

And we'll throw open the front door and rush in and look around. Nothing broken, nothing destroyed, nothing dusty or faded. Even the houseplants on the window sills have been watered. Up in my bedroom, Heidi is sitting on the shelf, smiling at me like always with her glass eyes and bright red lips. As if we'd never been away.

It was all just a bad dream.

Then I remember that I meant to tidy the food bag. Everything's all jumbled up together, the dirty knife and the clean tea towel, the apples and the eggshells. I feel my way over to the bag. I've decided to empty it out, then put back anything that belongs in there. That way, I'll find out exactly what we've still got to eat. I don't bother to empty the side pockets. They should still be tidy.

I kneel on the floor, turn the bag upside down to empty it, and pat the bottom.

I stop short. What made that clunk? The bag is empty now, so it must be something in one of the side pockets. I unzip them and slip my hand inside. My fingers feel a small metal tube.

What can it be? There's something sticking out from the side. It feels like a little switch. Can I move it? Yes, it slides sideways. As I push it, a bright circle of light appears on the ceiling.

Granny's flashlight!

Blinded, I half-close my eyes until they're used to the brightness. I shine the light around the room. Its beam flits over the three little ones, then comes to rest on Erwin. He's asleep, but not comfortably, with his back against the wall and his knees pulled up.

My heart is pounding in my ears. A flashlight! It would have been such a help all this time! I heard that metallic noise yesterday. Why didn't I check to see what made it? We'll only be here for another few hours now. It's hardly worth having found the thing.

All the same, a flashlight! I have to tell Erwin!

I stand up and walk over to him, enjoying the fact that I don't have to feel my way in the dark. I shine the light on the ceiling, the sink, the cracked mirror, the door to the main shelter, the cubicle doors. They're all battered and scratched! That's from hammering on them with the dustpan, but I don't care. We *had* to do it.

I shine the beam under the door of the left-hand cubicle. The broken glass glitters.

Erwin wakes up with a start when I shine the light on his face.

"Have they reached us?" he asks sleepily.

"Not yet, but we've got a flashlight!"

Astonished, he takes it from me and shines it around the room.

"This is great," he says delightedly.

He goes over to look up the shaft, then down at the floor. Right under the shaft, the tiles I swept this morning are thick with mortar dust again.

"They're digging up there," he says.

"Except," I say, "that they really ought to have signaled again long ago. It's been hours since we heard from them. Far longer than the other times!"

"That's only how it seems to you." Erwin waves his hand dismissively. It casts a shadow that dances across the wall. When is the last time we saw a shadow?

"You've got rings under your eyes," I tell him.

"So have you. You're all wrinkled, like Granny."

I take the flashlight from him, go over to the sink and peer at the mirror, but I can see almost nothing except a mosaic of cracked glass.

I go over to the food bag to see what I've emptied out: the rest of the broken cookies, three apples, two sausages and four boiled eggs. Erwin appropriates an egg and a sausage and drinks some water.

Poor Erwin didn't eat anything for supper. I'm overcome with a craving for an egg too, so I crouch down beside Erwin and peel it very slowly to make the pleasure last. I take tiny bites and chew them slowly, relishing their taste until, without thinking, I instinctively swallow them. No matter how slowly I try to eat the egg, and no matter how often I stop to lick my lips, it disappears.

"I'm still so thirsty," Erwin says with a sigh, wiping his mouth on his sleeve. "How much water is left in the tank?"

I don't know. I couldn't see in the dark and I didn't want to stick my grubby hand in it, but now we've got a light.

The broken glass in the left-hand cubicle crunches beneath our feet, although we try to walk softly. I climb up on the toilet and shine the beam into the tank. I can see the water level.

"There's maybe four or five mugfuls," I tell Erwin in a whisper.

"Then we could drink a couple, don't you think?" he whispers back.

My immediate reaction is to reject this idea as unfair. There are five of us. How could we possibly take half of the water for ourselves? It's tempting, though. The temptation grows until I can hardly think clearly.

"No," I say. "We'd have to leave most of the rest in the tank. It would be too hard to scoop it out."

"Still, we can afford a couple of mugs," Erwin repeats. I notice that he substituted "can" this time for "could." "We'll be out soon."

I hold my breath. "What if they don't get us out?"

"Then a little extra water won't save us."

I suddenly sense how parched I am. Erwin must be feeling the same. I push away my concern. Everything will be fine. They'll get us out all right—they know we're here. I dip the empty juice bottle in the water and fill it to the top. Our shadows dance across the walls as we leave the cubicle. It's selfish of us, I know, but I'm so tired of worrying about everyone else first! Why shouldn't I think of myself for once? Of *my* thirst?

Erwin obviously feels the same way. He stares at the bottle like a starving animal and almost snatches it from my hand. We pass it back and forth until it's empty.

My thirst is satisfied at last. I feel like a bloated sponge. Have I done a terrible thing, giving in to my desire for enough to drink? The same thought seems to be running through my brother's mind. We stare at each other.

"You're right," he mutters. "They've stopped signaling."

What does it mean? A wave of fear surges over me. We can't panic, whatever we do!

"It's nighttime," I say after a minute. "How can they work in the dark? They can't use floodlights because of the blackout."

That makes sense to him. He heaves a deep sigh. "What time do you think it is?"

I decide to modify my honest estimate—nine or ten o'clock—or the night will seem endless to him.

"Well after midnight," I hear myself say.

He sighs again, this time with relief. "It'll be light by eight o'clock in the morning. Then they'll start work again."

If they aren't going to signal during the night, and if I lie down really close to the younger ones, so I can hear if they get restless, I could have a bit of sleep too, couldn't I? Not a proper sleep, just a doze, so I don't miss the next signal.

"Get some sleep, Erwin," I say. "My turn to keep watch tonight."

He wraps himself in his blanket and lies down with his back against the sink wall, near the patch of new dust on the tiles beneath the window shaft.

"Why not come over here with us?" I ask.

"Because I'm closer to the window shaft here. They're bound to come through that way..."

I shine the light on him. He looks so alone there, and he hasn't even got a pillow. I slide the pack under his head. He's asleep instantly.

Have I thought of everything before the long night begins? Is there anything else I should do before I allow myself to doze off?

Then I remember Herr Rockel. I haven't told him about finding the flashlight.

I'd like to give him a nice surprise. He'll be amazed when he sees the light! I hold the flashlight against the mouth of the pipe and turn it on. A beam of light should be coming from the pipe and shining on the rubble in the men's room.

But there's no sound from the other side. Not a cough, not a shout. I switch off the flashlight and put it in my pocket.

"Herr Rockel!" I call into the pipe. "Hello! Did you see the light?"

I put my ear to the pipe and listen. Nothing.

"Say something, please!"

But there's no response. His breathing was so loud the last time. Now I can't hear a thing. What does it mean?

He hasn't eaten anything since the bomb fell. And all he's had to drink was a little watery elderberry juice.

"Would you like something to drink?" I call down the pipe.

There's only a couple of mugs of water left now—*if* we can scoop it up—and we don't know how much longer till they get us out. But if he answers, I'll gladly give him some. I'm already wishing Erwin and I hadn't drunk so much.

He doesn't answer, so he must be asleep—yes, he must be. If he's asleep, there's no point pouring anything down the pipe. It would only trickle down the other side of the wall again.

I use the toilet in the right-hand cubicle before lying down. The light makes it look bigger than it seemed before. Words and drawings have been hurriedly scratched or scrawled on the walls and the inside of the door. Mummy calls graffiti "filth" and expects me not to look at it. I've always obeyed her instructions till now, but for once I have a chance to look at my leisure.

A lot of them I don't understand. I peer at them more closely, trying to make out their meaning. Granny would shoo me out of the cubicle and say, "Darkness can be a mercy sometimes." Just once, it suits me that she isn't here. I want to form my *own* opinion about things. After all, I'm not a child anymore.

What's so "filthy" about "EDITH LOVES OSKAR"? Maybe Edith's boyfriend had left for the Eastern Front. Maybe she was missing him so much, she couldn't help expressing her love by scribbling on the wall. So what? And what am I to make of this picture here? A big fat elephant with wings and the name "WILLI" scrawled on its tummy. Beneath it are the words "I TAUGHT YOU TO FLY. YOUR LITTLE MOUSE." A mouse and an elephant? It sounds like a fairy tale. Are these the kind of ideas that occur to you when you're in love?

A shame that Gunther won't be in Dresden when we get there—Gunther, the curly-headed boy from the apartment below Grandpa and Grandma Glottke's. I used to play with him. We got along well. He's a year older than me—his birthday is only three days before mine, so he's already seventeen. But he's away in Chemnitz, serving as an anti-aircraft auxiliary, and he'll be joining the army soon.

I think he's a little bit in love with me. He's written me several letters from Chemnitz, one of them with a poem he wrote himself. I tried to think up a poem for him in return, but it never came to anything. The trouble is, I'm not really in love with him. I like him as a friend, that's all.

I go back to the children and lie down on my blanket beside Harald. It would be nice to go to sleep with the light on after so long in the dark, but who knows how long the battery will last? We have to economize on everything, even light. I switch it off and put it down within reach.

Now that I *could* go to sleep, I'm wide awake again. I snuggle up close to Harald. He's so nice and warm! I'm very fond of my little brother. He's quite different from Erwin, but I love them both in their own ways.

When the war is over, maybe I'll be able to visit the Rockels and make friends with Sophie. Sophie Rockel...I don't know her, but I like her already and I can't wait to meet her. I hope the war will be over soon. The first time I meet Sophie, I'll tell her all about these two nights we spent buried beneath the rubble, when her father was lying on the other side of the wall, badly injured and without even a blanket. And I'll tell her how we talked to him through the pipe and gave him something to drink, and how kind he was to us in spite of his pain.

Do you have a favorite poem, Sophie? Mine is Theodor Fontane's "John Maynard," or has been ever since we learned it in class…

I SIT UP WITH A JERK and turn on the flashlight. What time is it? I have no idea how long I've been asleep. I've lost all track of time and can't even make a guess. Herr Rockel would be able to tell me, if he's awake.

Very quietly, I get to my feet and steal over to the pipe. In a low voice, so I don't wake the others, I call: "Hello! Herr Rockel, are you all right? Can you tell me what time it is?"

He doesn't reply. Not a whisper, not a sigh, not the faintest sound of breathing.

I'm freezing cold. I crawl back under my blanket, shivering violently.

He must be dead.

18

I PICTURE HIM STRETCHED OUT beside the wall with his head near the pipe and his shattered leg lying limp on bloodstained tiles. And, looming around him, a mound of rubble. No soft deathbed for Herr Rockel.

Oh, Sophie, if you saw your father lying there like that!

And my father? Maybe it's the same with him. Mummy got his last letter ten days ago—no, twelve. If the worst happened, would we ever find out how and where he died?

I turn off the flashlight to save the battery—it certainly won't last the whole night. But now I see Daddy the way I saw him in my dream. He's a more horrible sight than Herr Rockel next door. My Daddy, all cold and bloody and lifeless...

No, he *can't* be like that, I won't let him be!

And what about me, about us? If they don't get us out, it won't be long before we're lying here in silence too. We've hardly got anything left to eat. And only a couple of mugfuls of water, maybe...

Dead. Not being there anymore. No, not that, not that! I clamp my hand over my mouth to stop myself from crying out. I don't want to die!

I try to force myself to think of something else. It'll be my birthday soon. Or is it my birthday already?

Grandpa and Grandma Glottke are sure to be worried about us, since we didn't get there when they expected us to. What if we didn't have them, what then? At least we'll be able to stay with them in Dresden until we can go home again.

Daddy and Mummy and Erwin and I went to stay with them before Harald was born. That was before the war. I must have been eight or nine. We went to the city center, me holding Mummy's hand and Erwin on Daddy's shoulders. The streets were swarming with men in uniform and there were swastika flags flying everywhere, because Hitler was visiting Dresden. Daddy and Mummy were anxious to see him. I saw him too. He was standing on a balcony, raising his right arm again and again as the banners and soldiers paraded past him. We couldn't get close to him because everything was roped off and policemen were holding the spectators back. I thought Hitler looked like any other man, but when Mummy waved like crazy and Daddy and the rest of the crowd shouted "Heil!" at the tops of their voices, I realized that Hitler must be someone very special, after all.

In those days Daddy and Mummy never dreamed that Hitler would start a war, let alone that they would end up on the losing side.

MAYBE IT REALLY IS AFTER MIDNIGHT? Impossible to be sure.

I sneeze suddenly. I'm so cold.

They'll get us out today if we're lucky. What about Herr Rockel? Will they get him out too? So many people may have been buried alive that the rescue teams will have more than enough to do to rescue *them*. They might not bother about the dead.

Will Sophie only hear about her father's death and his last day from me?

I turn on the flashlight again. The light seems far less bright than it was. Rolfi stirs and whimpers in his sleep. I put the light under my blanket but leave it on. Carefully, without pulling the blanket off the other two, I pick up my little brother and carry him into the cubicle with my cheek against his. His diaper is still dry, so I don't have to change him.

I suddenly think about the new baby. Mummy said one time that she was always the fondest of whichever one of us needed her the most. So she must now be fondest of my new brother or sister, a refugee child born in a strange town far from home.

That makes me think. What if Mummy had been buried with us down here and had to give birth to the baby in this ladies' bathroom, with nothing but a little water from the tank to drink and wash with? Was it a blessing in disguise that she had to leave the train? I remember another one of Granny's proverbs: "There's nothing so bad that it couldn't be worse..."

It occurs to me, as I'm returning from the cubicle to our sleeping spot, that this room looks almost cozy in the soft light. I've got to know it even better than our own home.

"Rolfi," I whisper in Rolfi's ear as I lay him gently down again between Harald and Lotte, "you're the dearest, best little boy in the world..."

Mummy always says that when she has to get him out of his crib in the night, so he knows the words.

I turn off the flashlight but leave it under the blanket. I can hardly stand the darkness now. Has midnight come and gone? Is it already two or three hours into the new day, my birthday?

There's something the matter with me. I'm sweating now. My forehead feels hot and my throat is sore. I know what it is: tonsillitis. I've had swollen tonsils before. The floor was too cold. I hope I don't make the others sick. That's the last thing we need!

Dear God, I think, please let them get us out of here tomorrow. Don't let anything happen to prevent it. It isn't just any old day, after all, it's my birthday. Let me survive, me and everyone I love. That's my only birthday wish...

I'm standing on the mound of snow beside the station's main entrance. Beyond me is the concourse and the clock. I've no idea why I'm standing here or why and how I got here. I gaze out across the plaza, an expanse of grimy, trampled snow. An occasional snowflake comes drifting down.

Shouldn't there be some tall buildings on the other side of the plaza? Buildings five or six stories high, with rows of shop windows on the ground floor and billboards on the fronts? All I can see are blackened ruins jutting above a wasteland of rubble.

And I'm all by myself. No Mummy, no Granny, no brothers, no luggage.

I see, when I turn to look at the clock in the concourse, that there's not much left of the station either. But the trains are still running. I make my way to one of the platforms, where a small train is standing—just a locomotive and two cars. I get in, and the train sets off. It dawns on me that I'm in the local train that runs between our village and the county town. I can see the road beside the track, which is flanked by apple trees. I make out the pine woods, the low hill where the church stands in its graveyard, the Kropps' paddock with its wire-mesh fence, the alder-fringed stream, the village pond.

But the village itself is gone. Not even the church is still standing. The village hall and the fire station aren't there, and neither is the school, or the village inn, or the Kropps' and the Häuslers' farmhouses.

Our house isn't there either. Just the apple trees and the garden fence.

But Bella is sitting outside our garden gate. She turns her head in the direction from which I always came home from school, waiting...

A feeling of infinite sadness overwhelms me, drowning me in despair.

I SIT UP WITH A START. Total darkness. Where am I? It takes me a moment to remember. My head is throbbing, my throat feels raw, and my teeth are chattering with cold.

Then I remember: Herr Rockel is dead. I have to let Erwin know. He'll cope with the news all right, but I'll have to lie to Harald and Lotte.

"Gisel!" I hear him call softly. "They're signaling again!"

I nod, not that he can see me.

"Yes!" I call back.

I hear him returning their signal with the broomstick, tapping in threes again. The other kids are stirring now too. I hear their sleepy voices calling me. They're thirsty, they say.

I must get up and go to them.

"Come on, Gisel," Erwin calls impatiently. "Let's have some light!"

Oh right, the flashlight. I find it under my blanket. So that was what kept digging into me. I turn it on. The bulb glows for a brief instant—Harald and Lotte exclaim in delight—then there's a tiny click and it goes out. We're in darkness again.

"Has the bulb gone kaput?" Erwin asks.

"Looks like it."

"What bad luck!"

"What was that light?" Harald asks.

Should I tell them about finding the flashlight last night, when they were asleep? They'd be excited, then disappointed when they hear that it won't work anymore. No, I'll spare them that.

"It was a signal from up above," I say. "It means we'll be out of here soon."

"That can't be right," Lotte says. "There'd have to be a hole in the ceiling."

"Maybe there already is one," says Harald. "It's just that we can't see it unless they shine a light. We'll have to look up fast next time they do."

"They won't shine a light again," I tell him. "We know they're coming."

I pick up Rolfi and send Harald and Lotte off to the toilet. That'll keep them busy while I tell Erwin that Herr Rockel is—

"It stinks in here!" Lotte protests.

I can't smell a thing, my nose is all stuffed up. The two of them start arguing over who goes first.

"Honestly," Erwin sighs, "if the stink could kill us, we'd be dead by now."

Dead...The word is like a knife thrust. My thoughts pass through the wall to where Herr Rockel is lying. I pick up the children's blanket and take it over to the sink side of the room. I don't want them lying near a dead man, even with a wall between them. I also bring my own blanket, along with the food bag and the makeshift pillows.

"Erwin?" I say, groping my way toward him.

He merely grunts. The loss of the flashlight has depressed him. It doesn't affect me much because my head is buzzing and I can hardly swallow.

Then we hear something that lifts our spirits.

"Can you hear it too?" Erwin exclaims. "Something's going on up there!"

A DULL SOUND PENETRATES THE CEILING, a series of rumbling, drilling noises, sometimes louder, sometimes softer. Everyone's listening. Even Harald and Lotte have fallen silent.

"Have they broken through already?" Harald calls.

"It'll take them a while longer," Erwin tells him.

Their bickering resumes.

I feel as if I'm floating and have to hold onto the wall, I'm so dizzy all of a sudden. It's lucky Erwin can't see me.

The voices from the toilet grow louder, so I have to go and settle the argument. "In order of age, you two! Lotte first, then Harald!"

As soon as they're finished I hold Rolfi over the toilet bowl. His diaper's still dry, so I've timed it right. I feel so faint, once I've pulled up his layers of clothing and buttoned him up, that I have to shut the lid and sit down. This toilet is our only seat apart from the one in the cubicle next door, but that's full of broken glass.

I remember that it's my birthday. Could that be part of the reason I'm feeling so strange?

So now I'm truly sixteen years old. When I get back to the surface I won't be the same as I was the night before last. I'll be two nights and days older—"more mature," as Granny might say. I can now think about Herr Rockel lying dead next door without feeling scared. Even if I hadn't found that flashlight or Granny hadn't put it in the side pocket, I *still* wouldn't have lost all hope.

Rolfi is growing impatient. He's banging on the cubicle door.

"Where are you, Gisel?" I hear Harald call. "We're hungry!"

I drag myself out of the cubicle and feel my way over to the food bag. All it contains are some bits of cookie, the last sausage, two eggs and three apples.

"You share it out," I tell Erwin wearily, handing him the food. "And help Rolfi. I don't want anything."

I can hear Erwin busying himself beside me. Presumably he's dividing up the sausage, eggs and apples so he can hand them out.

"Erwin..." I whisper.

No, Harald and Lotte are too close, they'd hear. I can't tell him yet. Besides, he's busy with the food.

"Is that all?" Harald exclaims disappointedly.

"It won't be much longer," Erwin tells him with his mouth full. "If you stuff yourself down here, you won't have any room for all the scrumptious things they'll give us to eat when we get out."

He turns to me. "Did you ask Rockel the time this morning?"

"No." I feel my eyes fill with tears.

"Did you forget?"

"Erwin," I whisper, "there's something I have to—"

The rumbling, scraping noises above our heads increase in volume—they sound much closer. Erwin jumps up. I hear him shuffle over to the pipe.

"Hello!" he calls. "Can you hear that racket overhead? It won't be long now!"

Everyone listens, waiting for Herr Rockel to answer. Everyone but me.

"Herr Rockel?" Erwin calls again. Then he comes back.

"How on Earth can he sleep through this?" he says. "Anyone would think he didn't care if he's rescued or not."

I should tell him now, but it's all I can do not to burst into tears. Besides, Harald and Lotte are thirsty—they're demanding something to drink. I take the bottle and mug and feel my way into the left-hand cubicle, broken glass crunching under my feet.

What am I doing in here? I can't remember. I sink down on the toilet seat and sit there, staring into the darkness.

"Gisel?" Erwin's voice seems to come from far away. "Need any help?"

I sigh. "No thanks, it's all right."

Now I remember. I climb carefully up onto the toilet lid and lay the bottle down in the bottom of the tank. Hardly any water goes in. I'll have to bail it out with the mug, but the neck of the bottle is so narrow. I have an idea: I stand the bottle upright in the tank.

That raises the water level a little, and any water I spill will run back into the tank, so none will be wasted. I bail and pour, bail and pour. The water that trickles into the bottle gets less and less, I can tell from the sound.

I have to stretch to reach the very bottom of the tank. My arms are so tired, I feel like yanking the whole thing off the wall!

The noises overhead are getting even louder. Boom, boom! But they're nothing compared to the noise the bomb made.

"There's some plaster trickling down!" Erwin calls excitedly. "Bits of mortar, even!"

All the same, we could be here for a long time yet. They won't be through until big chunks of concrete start landing on the floor.

I go on bailing, although only a thimbleful of water goes in each time I empty the mug into the bottle.

"Leave it," Erwin calls. "The last bit doesn't matter, we'll be out of here before much longer."

I pick up the bottle. It must be about three-quarters full, judging by the weight. To check how much is left in the tank, I stick my finger in the water. It only comes up to the first knuckle.

I climb down stiffly onto the heap of broken glass. The crunching noise is a signal.

"The water's coming!" Lotte shouts.

"Water!" Harald cries delightedly.

They hurry in my direction. Misjudging the distance in the dark, they blunder into me and knock me back against the cubicle door. The bottle slips through my fingers, hits Harald on the side of the head and smashes on the floor.

Harald starts crying, and the others freeze in horror. So do I. If we weren't able to get out of here soon, that would have meant our certain death. For a second I feel angry with Harald and Lotte, but that's ridiculous. It was an accident, and there'd be more water if Erwin and I hadn't drunk so much last night. My throat is so sore now, I don't think I could drink anything today anyway, but it's going to be very hard on the others.

"Careful," I call, "there'll be broken glass all over."

Then I hear someone sweeping up the mess. It must be Erwin.

"I'm shoveling it into the left-hand cubicle," he announces. "Watch the puddle!"

I hear Rolfi calling me. Erwin probably put him down on the floor near the sink, but he's not staying there.

"Gisel!" I hear him call. "Gisel!"

Not "Gille" anymore? That's something new he's learned down here!

"Rolfi," I call back, "you just said my name properly!"

He comes toddling toward me. I grope for him in the dark. Where in heaven's name is he?

I nab him just before he reaches the puddle. He lets out an indignant yelp. Harald, still crying, insists that I feel the bump on his head. How many bumps on the head has he had since we left home? Incredible, the amount of punishment he absorbs!

I drag Rolfi away from the puddle. Then I bend down, moisten my fingers in the water and lay them on Harald's bump. The cold is soothing and he stops crying.

"Are you going to get some more water, Gisel?" Lotte asks in a timid voice.

"There isn't any left," I reply wearily.

"But I'm so thirsty!"

"We're all thirsty."

She starts sniffling.

"They'll dig us out soon," I say as cheerfully as I can. "Then we'll get as much to drink as we want."

"But they're taking so long."

"Not half as long as we've already been down here."

That doesn't help. Rolfi starts crying too. He probably senses that we're all upset. I pick him up and cuddle him. I'm shivering with cold. If only the time would pass quicker!

Harald asks me what time it is. I can't tell him.

"I'll go ask Herr Rockel," he says brightly. "Perhaps he's woken up."

"No!" I shout. "Leave him alone!"

Harald falls into startled silence. He isn't used to me shouting.

Someone sneaks up to me. It's Erwin.

"Let me whisper in your ear," he says softly.

What does he want? I put Rolfi down but keep hold of his hand, and tilt my head. Only a little, because Erwin is almost as tall as I am.

"You don't think he's...?" he whispers, so softly that the others can't hear, with his hand cupped round his mouth.

I let go of Rolfi and hold Erwin's head in both hands—gently, so I don't poke him in the eye by mistake. Then I move so my mouth is close to his ear.

"Yes," I whisper, fighting back tears. "He stopped breathing during the night."

Rolfi is crying bitterly now, almost as if he understood what I just said.

"What's wrong?" Lotte calls. "What's the matter with Rolfi?"

"He's hungry and thirsty," I tell her, my throat tight. "But our rescuers will break through any time now."

"You keep saying that," Harald grumbles. "You've been saying it since early this morning."

Early this morning? It seems only an hour ago, two at the most. But who knows, maybe it's already noon?

19

SOMEONE IS DRILLING THROUGH THE CEILING. No, through the rubble over the window in the shaft. The noise grows louder and louder. I've picked Rolfi up again. He's clasping me around the neck with both arms, scared by the racket. We all stare up, hardly breathing.

There! There! A small round hole appears above the window grille. It's the mouth of a pipe. A narrow shaft of light slants down, too faint to brighten the room. Is it daylight? No one whoops for joy. We just stare up in stunned silence.

"Hello?" A man's voice. It seems to come from a long way off, so we hear it only distantly. "Anyone there?"

"Yes, five of us!" Erwin yells. "Eighteen months, six, seven, twelve and fifteen!"

"Sixteen!" I call.

Erwin glances at me in surprise.

"No adults?"

"There's a man next door," I shout, "but—"

"Call him!"

"No point," Erwin shouts. "He's dead!"

Too late. Now the others know.

"But he isn't dead!" Lotte protests.

"Yes, he is," I tell her. "He died last night."

She bursts into tears.

"Have you felt his pulse?" the man calls down.

"We can't get to him," Erwin replies. "He's on the other side of the wall!"

It takes a while to explain that we're in the ladies' bathroom and he's in the men's room. And how we talked through the pipe...

A pause. We hear the man talking to someone else. Then:

"What about you? Anyone hurt?"

"No, we're all fine."

"We're thirsty, though!" Harald puts in.

"And hungry," Lotte sobs.

"Don't worry, we'll get you out of there soon!"

The man asks so many questions: what our names are, where we're from, where our parents are. Erwin and I take turns answering.

Why all these questions? He's only wasting time!

Then a woman calls down to us: "Gisel? Erwin?"

We know that voice! It's...

"Granny!" we yell. Lotte joins in. Although we can't see her—the pipe is far too narrow—we can hear her sobbing. My eyes are brimming with tears.

"Thank God!" she calls in a choked voice. "Is Rolfi there too?"

"Shout 'Here!' Rolfi," I tell him. I point to the hole, but the shaft of light is so faint that my arm is barely visible.

"Here," Rolfi says.

Although he doesn't shout the word, Granny must have heard him. It wouldn't surprise me if she's lying on her stomach to get as close as she can! "Oh, thank God you're all safe!" we hear her say, then a confused murmur of voices.

"Marta!" Lotte calls. "Marta, are you there too?"

No answer. She bursts into tears.

"Call to your Mummy," I tell her, but she shakes her head.

"Don't cry, Lotte," Harald whispers, giving her a hug.

I put my free arm around Lotte, sorry for her, but thrilled to think that someone is eagerly waiting for us up there.

Granny...She must have taken refuge in another air-raid shelter when she couldn't find us inside the station. Then, when she still couldn't find us after the all-clear went, she must have been so worried!

Never mind, we'll all be together soon. Then we'll go to Dresden and everything will be...

What about Mummy and the baby?

"Listen, kids," someone calls down, "be patient just a little longer. There's still some rubble to be cleared, but we'll have you out soon."

"We need water!" I call. "We're terribly thirsty!"

Indistinct mumbling, then: "Have you got something to catch it in?"

"Yes!" I shout.

"Then get it. Yell when you're ready."

One of the bottles was smashed, but we still have the other one—it's in the bag. I pass it to Erwin, my hand is trembling so much, and sit Rolfi down beside the bag.

"Stay there," I tell him firmly.

"The bottle's no good," Erwin says. "We need the mug."

The mug...I had it with me before, when I came out of the cubicle.

"Find the mug," I call. "It must be somewhere here."

Everyone starts searching. I hear Erwin shuffling through the puddle on the floor. Then there's a clatter and I hear the mug rolling across the tiles. I feel for it with my foot, bump into Harald and Lotte and almost trip over Rolfi, who hasn't stayed where I left him. I have to grab him before he crawls into the puddle.

Harald holds out the mug and I grope for it. I've gone from cold to hot, and sweat is trickling into my eyes, but I don't care.

"Ready!" Erwin calls. We hold the bottle and the mug under the hole.

Water comes gurgling down the pipe. Erwin tries to catch the thin trickle in the bottle while I hold the mug underneath to catch what he misses, but most of it lands on the floor. I hear it splashing as it forms a new puddle. The trickle dries up.

Erwin shakes the bottle to check how much water is in it. Almost none, and there's barely a mouthful in the bottom of the mug.

"Did you catch enough?" a man's voice asks.

"No, hardly any!" Erwin calls back. "We've only got a bottle and a mug, and it's dark in here!"

More murmurs.

"Gisel," Granny calls down, "isn't there any cleaning equipment down there? There might be a bucket somewhere."

The bucket! Why didn't we think of it before? I feel my way past the cubicles to the broom closet and pull out the bucket. It smells a little, and I'm sure it isn't too clean, but it should be safe enough. Erwin calls for water again. By the time it stops, the bucket is a good one-third full.

"Hang on, kids!" the voice calls down. "We won't be much longer." Then another voice adds: "Move as far away from the shaft as you can! We don't want any debris landing on your heads!"

"Understood!" Erwin calls back.

The bit of light vanishes, and the rumbling, scraping sounds resume. We go over to the wall between the sink and the door, where the tiles are dry, and sit down side by side. Rolfi clambers onto my lap.

I dip the mug in the bucket again and again and let the others drink as much as they want. Listening to them, I realize how parched and painful my throat is. When they've all had enough I take a swallow. It hurts at first, but the water is icy cold and numbs my throat. Water has never tasted better.

We're back where we were sitting right after the bomb exploded: beside the wall between the door and the sink, with our backs against the radiator. Two days ago the radiator was hot; now it's freezing cold. I'm sitting with Rolfi on my lap, Lotte snuggled up against me on the left and Harald on my right. Is there anything I should think of, anything to do but wait?

My head is buzzing, my temples are throbbing. If only it were all over!

Suddenly something falls down the shaft and lands with a crash—something heavy, not small fragments.

"Hear that, Gisel?" Erwin says exultantly.

"Put the blankets back in the pack," I mumble. And our food bag?

Is everything stowed inside it that should be in there? I suddenly remember the mug and the bottle. Where are they? I can't think straight.

Erwin is looking after everything. I hear him moving around the room, hear objects clinking, then the purr of a zipper being closed. A moment later Erwin crouches down in front of me. I feel his hand on my arm.

"Happy birthday," he says.

"What?" Harald exclaims. "Is it your birthday today, Gisel?"

He reaches for me in the dark—his finger pokes me in the eye and makes me see stars—then hugs me tight. Rolfi grumbles, not knowing what's going on. Lotte hugs me too. Then Erwin and Harald sing "Happy Birthday."

Almost simultaneously the noise overhead doubles in volume, drowning their voices. More crashes and bangs and drilling. We listen without talking, hoping. Hurry, come quick!

Oh, Granny, my throat is so sore, it hurts when I swallow. I'm feeling limp, too. If only we were together now. Then all my worries and responsibilities would be over...

"I'm so cold," Lotte complains.

"Me too," says Harald.

So am I. We aren't moving around anymore.

"Get the blankets, Erwin," I say.

"I've just put them away," he protests. "It wasn't easy, stuffing them into the pack. Get them out again? No. If you're cold, too bad. I'm taking it easy for a bit."

"We'll get them ourselves," Lotte says. "Come on, Harald."

They won't be able to get the string open, they'll get it in a knot.

Any minute they'll be calling me...

But they don't—they even flap a blanket in my face. "Would you like one too, Gisel?" I hear Harald ask.

Oh, yes, I would. It's wonderful to be looked after. I feel the blanket being draped over Rolfi and me. My bottom is freezing. I push one corner of the blanket under it. It feels so soft and comforting. "Thank you, Granny..."

"I'm not your Granny!" I hear Lotte giggling.

What did I say? Was I dreaming?

The noise is so loud now that it drowns out every other sound. The broken glass in the left-hand cubicle tinkles because the whole room is vibrating from the equipment. It's good I've got Rolfi on my lap. I can tell from the feel of him that he's sleeping peacefully. In this pandemonium!

Is Erwin asleep too? I couldn't hear his breathing if I tried. A hand brushes my cheek. Someone is feeling for me.

"Who's that?" I call.

"Me!" Harald yells in my ear. "They're taking so long! Tell us a story, Gisel!"

In this racket? I'd have to shout my head off.

The noise becomes deafening, I have to put my fingers in my ears. Is that a pneumatic drill? Then all of a sudden—I have no idea how long we've been straining our eyes in the darkness—huge chunks of concrete rain down and a big hole appears in the ceiling. I shut my eyes, blinded by the light flooding in. Rolfi starts wailing—the din has finally woken him up, and no wonder.

"They're through at last!" Harald yells, throwing his blanket aside.

An incredibly fresh, cold gust of air blows in on us. The noise dies away. I open my eyes again—gradually, because the glare is painful. Erwin leaps to his feet and runs over to the shaft. I see the empty backpack lying on the floor and beyond it the food bag with the zipper shut. Beside me, Harald has jumped up and is dancing around, chanting, "We're getting out! We're getting out!"

Lotte is standing beneath the big hole with Erwin. "Marta?" she calls timidly.

Everything happens very quickly after that. A ladder is lowered and a man climbs down it. Instead of announcing, "You're safe now!" or "You were lucky!" or "Your troubles are over!" he wrinkles his nose and says, "Phew, what a stench!"

Having helped Harald up the ladder, he picks Lotte up and passes her to someone overhead. While I'm slowly walking to the ladder with Rolfi in my arms, Erwin grabs the blankets, stuffs them back into the pack and hauls it over to the ladder, where the first man tosses it up to his partner. Erwin hands him the food bag too. That done, he climbs the ladder himself.

I take a last look around. The room looks very small. The puddle catches the light, and so does the broken glass glittering under the door of the left-hand cubicle.

The man isn't a man at all, I see now, but a boy not much older than myself. He's smiling at me. I realize that I haven't combed my hair today—or Lotte's either. How could I have forgotten?

"Brave kids," he says, taking Rolfi from me.

"Herr Rockel—that's the dead man—he's behind that wall," I tell him.

He nods. "We'll get him out too," he says. Then he adds, "Not that he's in a hurry anymore."

A second man is already climbing down the ladder armed with a pickax. His face is muffled up in a scarf. All I can see is a furrowed brow and a pair of bushy eyebrows.

"Up you go," he calls to me. "Your grandmother can't wait till you're all with her, safe and sound."

The boy starts up the ladder carrying Rolfi with one arm. My baby brother turns and holds out his arms to me, not wanting to be carried by a stranger. His red hat has slipped over one eye. I smile up at him and push it straight.

I hear exclamations of joy overhead. Granny, who has been hugging Harald and Erwin, reaches down and takes Rolfi from the young man. Behind me, I hear the tiled wall splinter under the blows of the pickax. Goodbye, Herr Rockel...

I gaze up at the brilliant blue sky.

It's utterly dazzling!

Brave? I don't think that's the right word. We just did our best to survive.

"Hurry up, young lady!" Several men are standing at the top, waiting for me to get up the ladder. "We've still got plenty to do."

"It's my birthday," I hear myself say.

20

My dear Stefanie,

I'm sure you'd like to know what happened after we were rescued.

Granny, with Rolfi in her arms, pulled me close and kissed the top of my head (my hair must have been a complete mess). All of a sudden, I couldn't help crying. Now that I wasn't responsible for the others, I could afford to let my tears flow freely. My knees gave way and I had to sit down on the rubble. Granny's eyes were moist too. She patted me and praised me and said my parents would be proud of me.

A Red Cross helper rested her hand on my forehead. "You should be in hospital," she told me. "You've got a high temperature."

But I didn't want to go to a hospital. I wanted to stay with Granny and the boys and travel on to Dresden with them.

All I saw at first, once I'd wiped away my tears, was the mound of rubble we were standing on—then I realized it was only one mound among many. At intervals between them were gutted buildings with empty windows, charred ruins in which fireplaces and the remains of floors and ceilings could be seen. Pictures and tattered strips of wallpaper still hung on the inside walls, and a flock of pigeons had taken up residence in a burned-out elevator. Sooty curtains fluttered in the breeze, broken pipes glinted in the sunlight. A wasteland of debris stretched away to the horizon. Here and there, thin threads of smoke were still rising into the air.

As shocked as I was by this terrible devastation, it seemed somehow familiar. Where, I wondered, had I set eyes on such a scene before?

Lotte's mother wasn't there, nor—of course—was Marta. She stood there forlornly, crying.

I heard a man's voice calling from below: "If those children are still around, take them away! They'd better not see this..."

"This" could only be Herr Rockel. I wanted to stay—wanted to see what he looked like, the man who had shared our hours underground—but Granny shepherded me away. A nurse took Rolfi from her and escorted us. Lotte came too, as if it was the most natural thing in the world.

We scrambled down the mound of rubble. I felt splintered roof tiles crunch beneath my feet and had to climb over some charred beams. The fire here must have been intense.

The alley leading to the street was strewn with debris. So was the street itself when we got there. A Hitler Youth detachment was busy clearing a path down the middle, though it was far too narrow for cars or horse-drawn vehicles. You could hardly tell it had been a street at all.

Was this really the same town in which we'd rushed from one air-raid shelter to another? People were clambering around among the ruins, presumably in search of missing loved ones or treasured possessions.

Rolfi, Harald and Lotte gazed around. Erwin and I were too awed to speak. Ahead of us lay the station plaza, a big, deserted expanse covered with a layer of soot-stained snow. The few people hurrying across it were carrying salvaged articles under their arms or on their backs: a hamster cage, a scorched quilt, some battered saucepans, a rocking horse. One woman was pushing a baby carriage.

The sight of it prompted me to break the silence. "Granny, have you heard any news from Mummy?"

She shook her head sadly. "I spent the whole time looking for you."

The station had received a direct hit. Half of the front of the building had disappeared—together with the mound of snow we'd been standing on—but trains were still running.

The nurse took us first to a Red Cross depot, which was very crowded. People who had lost their homes in the raid were sitting or lying around all over the place. We had to thread our way through them.

"All my children are buried!" a woman was moaning. "All of them!"

I discovered only then what time it was, having forgotten to ask anyone. A clock on the wall said nine minutes past one. We were offered as much rice pudding and stewed apples as we could eat, with lemonade to drink. Erwin, Harald and Lotte tucked in with a will, but I wasn't hungry, just dog-tired.

Two Red Cross volunteers took down our names. They questioned Lotte the most: How old was she, where did she live, and how had she become separated from her mother? I told them how we came to be together. They glanced at each other sadly but made no comment. They wanted to take charge of Lotte, but she clung to me, so I took her hand and told her she could stay with us for the time being.

"Yes," agreed Granny, "you can stay with us for now." And she gave the Red Cross women the address of her best friend, Anna Beringer.

That surprised me. "Why her?" I asked. "We'll be staying in Dresden with Grandpa and Grandma."

Then Granny told me what she had only found out a few hours ago, when she heard it from our rescuers: Dresden, beautiful Dresden, had been reduced to rubble.

"But what about Grandpa and Grandma?" I asked in horror.

Granny shrugged her shoulders and didn't reply, but I could tell from her expression that she didn't believe in miracles.

I was given some medicine for my fever. Granny told me later that, after hearing the awful news about Dresden, I pillowed my head on my arms and fell asleep in a flash.

A RED CROSS NURSE accompanied us to the station—needlessly, because all we had to carry were Rolfi, our empty food bag and the backpack. The two big suitcases were gone for good.

We caught a train that same afternoon, but we had to change five times because we were forced to make a big detour around Dresden. The station there was completely out of commission.

The trains were so jam-packed with refugees, we could hardly climb aboard and had to stand in the corridors or sit on the floor. At one station we had a four-hour delay, which we spent in a smoke-filled waiting room. At least it was warm in there. Granny carried Rolfi most of the time, because I was weak and my temperature was still rising. That journey to Bebra, in the middle of Germany, was hard for Granny.

She didn't even know if we would be able to stay with Anna, but Anna had always been a loyal friend, and she lived on a big farm inherited from her late husband.

Granny told me during the journey that she had thought of asking Aunt Gertrud, who was her daughter and Daddy's sister, and lived north of Dresden. Gertrud would certainly have taken us in for a few days, but all she had was a two-room apartment, and that would have been a tight squeeze. Besides, the town would have been in danger of capture by the Russians if they broke through, so she decided to take a chance on Anna.

One of the other things Granny told me on the journey was that—as I had guessed—she really had begun by hurrying to the main air-raid shelter. Alarmed when she didn't find us there, she tried to go and look for us elsewhere, but in vain: the air-raid wardens shut the door and wouldn't let anyone leave the shelter before the all-clear sounded.

After the all-clear she made her way to the other two public air-raid shelters, the ones we had run to, but both of them were buried. There were flames and clouds of smoke everywhere, and the firefighters and rescue teams had more than enough emergencies to deal with. At that point, Granny almost gave us up for dead. However, when she learned that people might still be alive beneath the rubble, she stayed. She spent the whole night roaming from one buried shelter to the other. Then, the next afternoon, it was reported that signals had been heard coming from our cellar, and rescuers set to work with an excavator and pneumatic drills.

We were the only people in our shelter to have survived. I learned much later that the air raid had claimed almost two thousand lives.

We finally got to Bebra on the evening of the day after my birthday.

From there we set off on foot for the village where Anna lived. Anna didn't recognize Granny at first, her face was so gaunt and grimy, but she was overjoyed when she did. She also said it was perfectly fine for us to have brought Lotte with us.

"One hungry fledgling more or less makes no difference," she said. "Besides, Gisela, Lotte wouldn't have survived if you hadn't taken her into the ladies' with you. Buried alive in the dark for two whole nights and most of two days—I doubt if you'll ever have a more memorable experience, and Lotte shared it with you. That forms a bond..."

Anna not only allowed us to stay but never expected any thanks for her generosity. Although she had already taken in a bombed-out family from a town near Germany's western border and a family of refugees from Estonia, she had two attic rooms to put us in. She baked me a big cake, so that we could celebrate my birthday after the event, and scrounged some diapers for Rolfi from her friends.

Anna has always seemed to me to be a perfect example of what it means to be a true friend.

Granny sent Aunt Gertrud a telegram telling her our address. She gave herself one day of rest; then she set off to find Mummy and the baby. Meanwhile, Anna looked after the younger children with my help. Luckily, I recovered from the tonsillitis fairly quickly, once I could rest. An express letter from Aunt Gertrud told us that she, too, was expecting to be evacuated at any moment.

Granny was very sad when she returned early in March. The town where she'd thought Mummy had gone had been occupied by the Russians, so she couldn't go there. She had looked for her in all the other towns on our route that she could reach, but without success.

THE WAR ENDED ON 8 MAY 1945, but it was July before Mummy rejoined us—alone. We hardly recognized her at first. Her hair had turned almost all gray, and she was little more than skin and bone.

It had been a difficult birth, and she hadn't managed to get away before the Russians occupied the town. And the baby? A girl named Erika, she had survived for only two weeks because Mummy was starving and unable to produce enough milk. There was no food to be bought during the last few weeks of the war and immediately after the fighting ended. Mummy had to bury our baby sister in a village graveyard, all by herself.

She couldn't write to Dresden because the front line ran between there and the town she was in, and there was no mail service in those first post-war weeks. As soon as possible after the war ended she set off for Dresden, where she expected to find Granny and us kids staying with her parents. No trains or buses were running, so she had to travel the whole distance on foot. Fortunately, it was summertime.

She couldn't walk lugging a heavy suitcase, so she exchanged my green birthday sweater for a backpack in which she stowed her bare essentials. Not knowing whether she'd find any help on the way, she traded the suitcase and the rest of her possessions for food.

She couldn't believe what people kept telling her—that Dresden had been completely destroyed by bombs—until she actually reached the devastated city. She managed to find her bearings, having been born and brought up there. When she finally came to the site of the apartment building where her parents had lived on the fourth floor, she found a gutted ruin. On the blackened wall, along with the names of many other former occupants of the building, someone had written in chalk:

FRIEDEL AND JOCHEN GLOTTKE: DEAD

"My legs simply gave way," she told us later, "and I sank down on a mound of rubble. Then I scrambled to my feet again because the names Gisela, Erwin, Harald and Rolf Beck weren't there."

From Dresden she trudged toward Aunt Gertrud's, because she assumed we must be staying with her. On the way she caught typhus and almost died. Gravely ill, she lay in a barn for two weeks. A kind old man who owned three goats brought her some milk morning and evening, and later on, when her strength was slowly returning, a few potatoes. She was so thin by the time she reached Gertrud's door that our aunt didn't recognize her at first.

"You're alive!" Aunt Gertrud exclaimed as they fell into each other's arms.

Mummy now knew that we and Granny were staying with Granny's friend Anna. After two days she set off again, this time for Bebra. She was able to catch a ride now and then on a farmer's wagon, but she walked much of the way.

And that was how she found us.

THE RED CROSS UNDERTOOK A SEARCH for Lotte's mother. Her father had been killed in action. Eventually they discovered that her mother had died in the same air raid that buried us alive. As for Marta, she couldn't be traced because Lotte didn't know her last name.

When Mummy reached Bebra, heard Lotte's story and saw how attached to us she had become, she said she was welcome to stay with us for the time being. And later on, when we learned that both of Lotte's parents were dead, she promptly offered to keep her until or unless some other member of her family was found.

Lotte's photograph appeared for years on Red Cross posters, along with her name, age and last known address. In those days, every town hall, railway station, post office and bank displayed posters of refugee children who had become separated from their parents. I always felt so sad for the children who had been lost as babies, and wondered what happened to them. Many of their photos said:

NAME: UNKNOWN. AGE: UNKNOWN.

All that was known was the place where they had been found.

No one ever came forward in Lotte's case. There were so many war orphans that the authorities were only too happy when a family decided to adopt one. I remember Mummy saying to me once: "Perhaps it was meant to be—perhaps Lotte is our replacement for Erika."

DADDY WAS HELD for a long time in a Russian prisoner-of-war camp. He had received no answers to his letters to Grandpa and Grandma Glottke in Dresden, so he wrote to his sister. After months of anxious suspense, he learned from Aunt Gertrud that Dresden had been destroyed, his parents-in-law were dead, and we were in with Anna. So he knew where to go when he was finally released. By then we had found an apartment of our own in Bebra, and Mummy was working as a kindergarten teacher, which she had been before she married Daddy.

My Daddy—your great-grandfather—developed kidney disease while he was a prisoner of war. You never knew him because he died before you were born, but he was always sick and irritable after his return home. Our post-war Daddy was very unlike our pre-war Daddy.

He got especially worked up whenever the conversation turned to our old province of Silesia, his homeland. After the war it became part of Poland, and all the German towns were changed to Polish names. Daddy never missed an opportunity to criticize the Poles, who were—in his opinion—ruining the place. Mummy, who took a completely different view, was in favor of reconciliation between Germans and Poles.

As soon as Germans were allowed to travel to Poland, we all paid a visit to our old home. The Polish family who now lived in our house were very friendly. They asked us in—even invited us to take coffee with them—and showed us around. The woman of the house told us that she originally came from western Ukraine, and that she had been deported from there. She and her family were allowed to take only what they could carry, so she knew what it was like to lose one's home. None of our things—the dishes, our books—had been left in the house. Someone else had probably stolen the valuable items, but by then it didn't seem so important.

Erwin, Harald and I got on well with the young Poles, as did Mummy with their mother. The only person who wasn't friendly was Daddy, who barely uttered a word. When we were back in the car again, he growled: "We're betraying our birthright, associating with those people..."

He and Mummy often argued about it. The fact is, the war had simply destroyed our poor, dear Daddy. Luckily, it wasn't until after his death that a letter came for Mummy from the Polish woman. She wrote that her son Jan had come across our old French clock while renovating the cellar, and that we were welcome to collect it if we wished.

So we went and collected it. Daddy would never have done that! To show our appreciation we invited the Polish family to visit us in Bebra. When they came, we didn't let thoughts of our "birthright" spoil their stay.

THERE'S ONE LAST THING TO TELL YOU. As soon as the mail service was more or less working after the war, Granny wrote to the authorities in Oldenburg and asked for the address of a family named Rockel, who lived at No. 14 in a street beginning with the letters "Ro." Several weeks later she received a reply that no one by the name of Rockel lived in Oldenburg.

I couldn't understand it, and neither could Granny. Why would Herr Rockel have given me an address that didn't exist?

A few years later, I discovered another Oldenburg in Germany. It's a small town northwest of the other Oldenburg, near the Baltic coast.

I didn't write this time. I went there in person during a university vacation. It was summertime, and I'd saved up a bit of money—just enough for the train fare. I didn't think about what might happen once I got there.

Sure enough, I found the Rockel family at No. 14 Rosenstrasse. The only people living there were Herr Rockel's widow and his youngest daughter, Sophie.

His army unit had notified them that he'd lost his life in an air raid, but they didn't know anything about how he died until I told them.

They wept, and I wept with them.

I was invited to stay for a few days. Sophie and I went to the Baltic coast, where we spent a day strolling along the beach. By the time we returned to Oldenburg, we were firm friends. And we have remained good friends our whole lives. Even though our homes are far apart, we call each other every week and exchange our news. We often talk about Sophie's father. He not only was important in her life, he means a great deal to me as well. He helped us survive those terrible hours underground. He gave us more than good advice, he gave us courage and hope.

Of one thing I'm certain: if I ever had to go through another experience as horrible as the last war, and if I and my grandchildren turned up on Sophie's doorstep one day, unannounced and without any luggage, she wouldn't hesitate to take us in and look after us to the best of her ability.

Every war is a crime, Stefanie. I wish we'd been spared the war I lived through as a girl, and I hope that you will never know what it's like to be involved in one. We must all do our best to create a peaceful society and ensure that monstrous crimes are never again committed in our name. Perhaps my story will show you that even ordinary people like us can be strong when we have to be. That's what really matters.

Your loving Grandmother

About the author

Gudrun Pausewang is a prolific, award-winning author and one of Germany's leading writers for teens. A passionate activist, her books focus on peace, environmental protection, and social justice.

Born in Germany in 1928, Pausewang is the oldest of six children. An eyewitness to the time period she writes about, she fled her own village at the age of seventeen.

After completing university, Pausewang worked as a teacher for many years. Her career began in Germany, but she also taught in Chile and Venezuela for a considerable period of time. She traveled throughout the region, as well as in North America.

Ms. Pausewang began her illustrious writing career in 1959. Her list of publications now exceeds 70 titles, many of which have been translated into other languages. She currently lives in Germany.